What Kind of FOOL

WHAT KIND OF FOOL

J.L. MINYARD

This book is a work of fiction. Names, characters, places, and incidents are either products of the author's imagination or are used fictitiously. Any semblance to actual persons, living or dead, events, or locales is entirely coincidental.

WHAT KIND OF FOOL © 2023 by Jessica Minyard

hello@jessicaminyard.com

Cover by Qamber Designs & Media

Editing by Erica Edits

http://www.ericaedits.com/

ISBN: 978-1-957004-06-8

eBook ISBN: 978-1-957004-05-1

20230912

Content Notes

This book contains material that may be sensitive to some readers. CWs: explicit sex and language, sexual and physical abuse (historical, off-page), abortion (historical, off-page), religious trauma, discussions of religion, alcoholism, anxiety, panic attacks (on-page), toxic family dynamics, estranged family.

National Domestic Violence Hotline
https://www.thehotline.org/
800-799-7233
Text START to 88788

For my sister, Katie.

You probably still can't read this one either. Sorry not sorry.

CHAPTER ONE
UNFINISHED BUSINESS

I was a cliché.

I stood there, hand on the gleaming silver steamer handle, re-making an angry white lady's drink because she swore I used coconut milk instead of almond.

I hadn't.

Five years as a barista and I knew how to making a fucking drink.

Couldn't tell Karen that, though.

So, I remade it in stormy silence while my coworkers gave me knowing looks and I daydreamed about art school.

A fucking cliché.

I whipped back around and handed her the hot drink with a winning, well-practiced smile. She took it, a fake designer bag swinging on her arm.

We held eye contact while she tasted the drink, holding up the afternoon coffee break line.

"Much better!" she exclaimed as she smacked her lips.

"Always happy to help!" I chirped in my customer service voice.

Alanna, the shift manager, sidled up to me, the copious amount of gold bangles on her arms clinking merrily. "Incoming. Your favorite customer."

She breezed away while I scanned the line in a panic, barely registering the next customer's extensive deviations from the recipe, Sharpie scrawling down his cup. I finally spied him, a few people deep.

Colton.

A white collar dudebro who worked in one of the large office buildings in the same strip as the coffee shop. I was used to seeing a lot of nine-to-fivers once or even twice a day as they went about their business. They were our regulars and biggest customer base. Most of them were perfectly pleasant and respectful of our parasocial relationship of customer and barista.

Not Colton, though.

Colton was some hotshot financial something or another and didn't let anyone forget it. Sometimes he came in alone, and sometimes he came in with a herd of other dudebros who all dressed the same in loafers, khakis, polos, and a branded company jacket and ID lanyard.

He was currently twirling his lanyard around in the air, heedless of other people around him. Part of me wished he'd smack someone with it so they'd smack him back. Hopefully.

Colton tipped relatively well and expected you to smile and laugh for him.

He had asked me out no less than five times and by the broad smile on his face as he approached the register, it seemed like today would be number six.

I'd hate to have to reject a guy six times.

When he made it to the front of the line, I hitched on my work smile and held up my Sharpie and a cup. I didn't usually oscillate between register and the machine, but we were training a new guy and he was woefully slow.

"The usual?"

He put his hand on the countertop and leaned against it, coming as close to my face as possible before hitting the register. His cologne was an overwhelming, sharp musk that caused me to lean back.

"Sheenah, don't be like that." He grinned, in what I'm sure he thought was a charming way. And he might be attractive and charming to the right girl, but not me. He was too slick and sly and his eyes were cold.

"Like what, Colton? There's a line." I gestured, in case he couldn't see it.

"I have two tickets to the concert downtown tonight," he said, as if he couldn't hear me. "One for the prettiest barista around."

I was seven hours into a ten-hour shift, so I honestly doubted that. Unless sweaty hair, smudged mascara, and coffee grounds-under-unkempt-nails were Colton's thing. Which was highly suspect, considering his head-to-toe branded clothes and accessories.

"I don't like music," I deadpanned.

He blinked a few times, processing this new information. "Everyone likes music."

"Not me." I wrote his name on his cup, as if *I* couldn't hear *him*. "The usual, then?"

He sighed dramatically, but finally lifted up from the counter and I felt the knot in my chest loosen.

"Only if you draw me a pretty picture."

Someone had let slip that I was an artist and ever since I'd been in charge of drawing on the billboards and people's cups, if they asked nicely. I was happy to do it for customers I liked, but unfortunately Colton wasn't one of those and also unfortunately he asked for one every time.

My fingers clenched around the Sharpie. It took all my effort not to scribble a tiny man on fire. Instead, I drew a standard pumpkin, since it was October, after all.

I did his standard pour and handed him the cup.

"What? No hearts?"

There was that grin again, the slick one, as he eyed my baggy black shirt, covered in splashes of milk and syrup. The way he just...lingered...made my stomach roil.

He tipped his cup at me.

"One day, Sheenah. One day, you'll say yes."

He finally walked away, but the sick, twisted feeling in my stomach stayed. I could feel the color draining from my face; the burn of bile rising up my throat. The Sharpie clattered to the counter as I dropped it.

Alanna's hand was on my shoulder and her soft touch brought me back to the present, back to the body that was only mine now.

"Sheenah, are you okay?"

I shook my head. "No, I need to go vomit."

It took almost ten minutes of me hugging the porcelain toilet before someone came to find me. I had my cheek pressed to the cool lid; I hadn't actually vomited. Just dry heaved into the toilet until the feeling passed. The handle jiggled, then I heard the key turn in the lock. Only Alanna had a key to the restrooms.

"Hey, Sheenah, are you okay?"

I nodded, still facedown.

"Colton's an idiot, but I didn't think he was really bothering you."

I heard the door snick shut and then Alanna crouched down into my line of vision.

Alanna was maybe twenty-five with sharp eyeliner and an English degree. She was the most popular manager because she always reminded us to take our breaks, rarely asked us to cover a shift, and was magnanimous with the bathroom key, to both employees and customers.

"Do you want me to call his boss?"

Alanna's offer was tempting, but I was already shaking my head. On the off-chance Colton's boss would actually do anything—other than immediately tell Colton—the brief flicker of joy it would bring me was not worth the risk, that I was sure of. Colton hadn't done anything other than be nauseatingly obnoxious. I hadn't seen him after work, as he had failed to follow through with any of his threats to meet me after my shift, and he hadn't tried to make contact on any social media.

Alanna frowned. "Are you sure?"

"I'll handle it," I said.

I wouldn't poke a sleeping bear because I knew how that story ended.

I finished up my shift without incident only twenty minutes late. I stuffed my soiled apron in the laundry basket in the back room, spritzed my chest with a light fragrance to try to cover up the smell of coffee grounds and milk, and hopped in my '96 Honda to trundle across town, hoping to be only a half hour late for my seven o'clock women poets class.

I had done two years at the community college for an Associate of Arts degree, but was now attempting to finish a bachelors at the satellite branch of Penn Warren University. The original plan was to room with my best friend Vivien at the main Penn Warren campus miles and miles away from here.

That was the plan. To hightail it out of this small town. That plan was torpedoed my senior year of high school and I had to stay behind and pick up the pieces of all my shattered hopes and dreams.

Only two semesters stood between me and a one-way ticket to the Southern Georgia School of Art and Design for my master's program.

I had to pass this poetry class, though. Poetry wouldn't have been my first choice, but I had delayed taking my Literature general education requirement for as long as possible and it seemed like the least painful option.

I was able to find a prime parking spot in the student lot—because only the truly desperate took seven o'clock two-hour-long classes—and pulled my phone out of my bag to turn it on silent. I had a couple texts from my fellow women poets victim, Rayme.

    Dr. Dickhead has noticed you're late
    Better hurry

I sent them back a couple crying emojis before stowing the phone away and locking up my car. Not that anyone would take two looks at the beater that barely got me around these days and think there was anything of value on the inside.

Dr. Dickhead was our not-so-secret codename for Dr. Howard, our professor, an average-looking white dude with a newly minted PhD who took points off an assignment if you slipped up and called him Mr.

Rayme and I had scored desks at the back of the class, and I slunk in as inconspicuous as possible. I had just slid into my desk when Dr. Howard said, "Nice of you to join us tonight, Ms. Barnes."

"Green-Barnes," I quipped. Rayme snorted into their textbook.

The marker he was using to write on the whiteboard screeched to a halt. *There go my attendance points for the day, stupid Sheenah.* But we were almost halfway through the semester. The least he could do was get my name right.

He looked at me over his blazer-clad shoulder, eyes narrowed. "You're late, Ms. Green-Barnes. Again."

I pulled my textbook and notebook out of my bag and arranged them quickly on my desk. "Sorry. Work ran over." I didn't bother to add a "won't happen again" because it definitely probably would.

He huffed but returned to droning on about how he just didn't understand women. No one else in the class gave our little drama any mind anymore. They were used to it. Dr. Howard had decided to make me his personal pet project because it irked him to no end that his class was not the number one priority in my life. He could get in line behind the job that paid my rent, my grad school application portfolio, and my tiny online business. I think he was also miffed that I was taller than he was.

Rayme was tapping their bedazzled stiletto nails on the desk, wearing a look of utter boredom. They were very high-femme today, with dramatic purple eyeshadow and matte purple lips.

I leaned over to get their attention and made a writing motion with my hand. Then mouthed, *Pen?*

Rayme grinned and handed me an extra. I grabbed it quickly while Dr. Howard's back was still turned.

It wouldn't do to let him know that I had arrived late *and* unprepared for class.

By the time I got home, it was nearly ten and I hadn't had any dinner yet. I popped a Lean Cuisine into the microwave and stared forlornly at the crowning jewel of my application portfolio—a high fashion, haute couture gown. I had been severely neglecting her since Vivien was in town a few weeks ago for the fitting. I had the measurements all down, but after the implosion and re-building of Vivien's love life, I'd had an epiphany about the design. So, it was almost back to the drawing board. I needed to get the dang thing finished so Vivien could come back and wear it to be photographed for my portfolio.

When the microwave beeped, I plopped the dinner down on the card table that served as my dining room table and dug in.

My apartment was a one-bathroom studio; the building they used was a converted elementary school that they had gutted and redone. It was barely in my budget, but beggars couldn't be choosers. I could survey all of my earthly belongings from the table. It wasn't much, but it was all mine and no one could take it away from me.

I didn't need much, anyway.

I had the studio space divvied up between my various projects—sewing and racks and dress forms in one corner, while the other was taken up by my easel and paints and a half-dozen unfinished canvases. I sighed. All my unfinished business haunted me day and night.

But I would worry about all of it later. Always later. A soul-deep tiredness had seeped into my bones, as it usually did after one of Dr. Howard's classes. My fingers ached and I couldn't even fathom touching a brush or sewing needle tonight.

Everything would have to wait until tomorrow. I had class in the morning and a shift at the coffee shop in the afternoon, but at least I didn't have Dr. Howard again until next week. I just had his research paper—which was worth thirty percent of our final grade—weighing down my bag and mind like a stone.

It would have to wait, like everything else.

I shucked my dirty clothes, showered with cool water because there was barely any hot water left at this time of night, and climbed into bed to sleep like the dead.

Chapter Two
BURRITOS

It was a very peaceful dead-sleep until I was woken abruptly by the pulsing of a bass above my head.

The music reverberated through my tiny studio; I could feel the damn bass line through my body.

What the actual fuck.

I pulled a pillow over my head and snuggled deeper into the covers. It didn't help. I grabbed my phone from the desk that also served as my nightstand and checked the time.

Two o'clock in the morning.

I was going to murder someone.

I grabbed my glasses and headed for the door. I wasn't really dressed for a confrontation—I slept in a ragged tank top and loose pair of sweats I'd had since high school—but it was two in the morning and I was exhausted.

Our building only had three floors so it wasn't hard to deduce where the racket was coming from. I had never heard noise like that coming from the floor above before. I didn't know many of my neighbors anyway so this was going to be one hell of an introduction.

I made it to the door of the apartment directly above mine—I could still feel the music, but it was less obnoxious out in the hallway. Lucky me.

I banged on the door so hard the handle rattled. Two of us could be assholes.

The music abruptly stopped and I heard the deadbolt turn before the door swung inside.

A man stood in the doorway, one of his large shoulders braced up against the frame. We were at eye level, so he wasn't more than six feet; six one would have been generous. He was shirtless and barefoot, a pair of gray sweatpants slung low over his hips. His chest and arms were all hard, sculpted muscle. They were covered in tattoos, from shoulder to wrists, of all different styles. And apparently designed by artists with very different skill levels. Some were obviously very talented and others were...very not.

"See something you like?" he drawled, his voice deep and decadent.

"Absolutely not," I snipped, before I could help myself.

I was pretty flat chested, which was why I was out braless in the hallway, but that didn't stop him from looking. Or keeping his eyes away from the exposed skin between my top and pants.

I tugged self-consciously on the hem of my tank top, even as I felt my face flush. "Do you have any idea what time it is?"

He grinned. "You came all the way up here in the middle of the night to ask me what time it is?"

He shifted, bracing his body harder against the door, the movement making his biceps and abdomen flex.

"It's two in the morning, I have to be at school at seven, and your obnoxious music woke me up."

"Oh, sorry." He at least had the decency to look contrite. "I didn't realize you'd be able to hear it. The muse strikes when the muse strikes, you know? You live downstairs?"

I resisted the urge to ask him what he was working on. I couldn't see much inside his apartment past his body. I wasn't here to make friends or small talk.

"Obviously."

His smile widened, as if my irritability was amusing to him. He was handsome, in a rough, rugged way, his brown hair cut short on the sides and a little bit of stubble lining his extremely square jaw. High cheekbones defined a thick, pouty mouth.

"What's your name, sweetheart?"

I bristled at the presumptuousness of the pet name. "That's none of your business."

"But it could be."

"*Absolutely* not."

And with my face flaming, I turned away and started back down the hallway, the flip-flops I'd thrown on echoing down the empty hall.

The noise wasn't loud enough to drown out his voice, though, as he said, "Good night, sweetheart," at my retreating back.

I had a hard time falling back asleep after the encounter with my new neighbor.

There was a tight, tingly sensation crawling under my skin. Something I hadn't felt in a very, very long time.

And what I was *absolutely not* going to do was masturbate to the idea of my hot upstairs neighbor.

My therapist would have a field day with that one. But I quit therapy. Because therapy was just another task on a never-ending list of tasks that I didn't have time for.

Get a grip, Sheenah.

Was I going to lose my mind because the hot neighbor looked at me?

Except he didn't just look at me.

His liquid brown eyes had *devoured* me. Like I was a snack. Like I was worth something.

So, I tossed and turned and tried to fill my mind with something else until my alarm finally went off at six.

I had my morning routine down to a science. I didn't have time to dawdle or make complicated decisions.

I packed an extra set of clothes in my backpack for work later and threw on a forest green, wide-legged jumpsuit over a long-sleeved black shirt.

The jumpsuit was the signature item from my online shop, A Siren Calls. It was fairly manageable to make a few at a time and it was easy to customize the colors and add embellishments to the straps. I could even remove the straps upon request without changing the pattern overly much.

I had started making my own clothes in middle school because it was an easy way to bond with my grandmother. My parents were also super religious and overly concerned with the length of my shorts and dresses, most of which were inappropriately short in my size. So, if I wanted to wear anything cute ever, at all, I had to learn how to make it myself.

I grabbed a few protein bars for the road, locked up, and headed downstairs to check the mail before I left for the day.

Our mailboxes were all gathered together in a little lounge area in the lobby.

I was in front of my box, keys jangling as I searched for the right one, before I noticed someone was occupying one of the chairs in the lounge.

I froze with my key in the lock, like a deer in headlights.

He popped up as soon as we made eye contact.

He was fully dressed this time, in tight, dark wash jeans, boots, a black shirt, and a black leather jacket. What? Was he part of the bad boys' club?

He was also holding up two cups of strong, black coffee. I could smell it.

"Were you waiting for me?" My pulse kicked up and the urge to panic was strong. *Relax.* "That's creepy, you know."

"Only for a minute." He held one of the coffees out towards me. "An apology coffee. For waking you up."

I could read B U R R on the knuckles of the hand that held out my apology coffee. He was smiling, but it was much more subdued than his wild smile of last night. Or, technically, earlier this morning.

I didn't make any moves to grab the drink.

"It's not poisoned, I promise. See?" He tipped his own drink towards his lips. I caught I T O S across the knuckles of his other hand.

I choked on a half laugh. "Do your hands say burritos?"

He tipped his coffee towards me. "They do indeed. I'm Snake, by the way."

I finally reached for the coffee, grabbing it quickly and delicately so as to avoid brushing his fingers with mine. I was not going to refuse a free coffee. If it was poisoned, at least I wouldn't have to finish Dr. Howard's term paper.

I blew on the lid before taking a tentative sip. I resisted the urge to sigh. Coffee really was the nectar of the gods.

"Is that your legal name?"

He chuckled. "No. But it's what everyone calls me besides my mother." Snake raised an eyebrow. "Are you really not going to tell me yours?"

I saluted him with the coffee. "Nope."

He just grinned, those deep eyes lighting with amusement. "Until next time, then, neighbor."

I managed to make it through most of the day without thinking about Snake and his eyes and his coffee or the way his fingers flexed around the coffee cup.

What kind of name was Snake, anyway? What kind of man got *burritos* tattooed across his hands for all the world to see? I liked burritos as much as the next person, but not quite enough to have them immortalized on my body.

Why was I spending so much time caring about what he did or didn't do? It was none of my business just like my name was none of his.

My therapist would ask why I felt the need to be so adversarial to people I didn't really know. If I kept them at a distance, then they couldn't hurt me.

I managed to make it through another day that was much the same as the rest.

I splurged for dinner and got takeout on the way home from work so that I didn't have to eat another frozen dinner.

I ate my dinner while watching a rerun of *The Great British Bake Off*, so I could be even more depressed about my lack of culinary skills and pastries.

After dinner, it was time to check my online shop for orders.

I was being very selective these days on orders and customizations. Not that I had a plethora of people beating down my door, because I was so inconsistent on Instagram when it came to promoting my brand.

I'd get an influx of requests anytime Vivien wore one of my pieces and tagged me in her posts. I tended to save my energy for those customers and not worry too much about the downtime between orders.

I had one order for a green jumpsuit and a chunky, pumpkin orange scarf. My scarves were very popular during this time of the year as people were getting their winter gear ready for the colder months. Plus, they made great gifts for those who were on a quest to shop small and local.

Lucky me, I had both of the items in stock. I printed the order information and shipping label, and went rummaging around my studio for shipping supplies.

Shipping supplies were so expensive to stock, so I usually tried to recycle and reuse as much as I could.

I managed to scrounge up an old shopping box and some packing confetti I had left over from a special sale a few months back. I even threw in a fat little crocheted bumble bee to sweeten the happy mail.

I had my TV volume down low; low enough that I could hear it drone on as background noise, but not up loud enough where it was distracting. I had to have some kind of background noise on or I tended to just start talking to myself if the room got too quiet.

Perks of spending so much time by myself, I guess.

I also happened to keep an ear peeled for any disturbances from upstairs. It wasn't quite the middle of the night yet, so maybe that was yet to come.

I could hear some scuffling across the floor and then I realized I had stopped what I was doing in order to listen.

"Creepy, Sheenah, creepy," I muttered, smoothing down the packing tape I had just meticulously laid across the seams of the box I was packing.

I would never have to see Snake again so I wasn't sure why I was wasting so much time thinking about him. I doubted he kept regular business hours, and I was gone most of the day every day anyway.

I finished my box and put it by the front door in the hopes I would remember to grab it and drop it off at the post office in the morning and not let it sit there for five days as I kept walking past it.

I ground my teeth together. I was already feeling anxiety about the damn box even though it should be a thing I could cross off my to-do list.

The interactions with Snake had really thrown me for a loop, apparently. I rubbed the spot on my sternum, as if that could clear the weight off my chest.

People are allowed to be nice to you, Sheenah, without ulterior motives.

But are they really nice, though?

I wanted to unload everything spiraling through my brain onto someone, anyone. I could feel the thoughts building and building on top of each other, like a well-laid wall of bricks. That could topple and crush me at any time.

I collapsed on my threadbare thrift sofa and hung my head between my knees. My hands fisted in the fabric of my sweatpants until the knuckles were white.

I focused on my breathing. The rise and fall of my chest. I visualized the air entering my throat and traveling down to my lungs. Visualized my lungs expanding and contracting with the effort to breathe. I visualized the air powering everything else in my body. Every muscle, every synapse.

Breathing was everything.

Breathing was life.

It was almost as if I could feel the blood slowing down in my veins; my pulse stopped racing; the weight eased from my chest.

I rubbed my fingers across my forehead and they came away damp with sweat. Great, just great.

A cold shower could do wonders, though.

I pulled all my hair back into an extremely messy bun in order to keep it as dry as possible and then went through the motions of getting into the shower.

I opened a new bottle of my favorite shower gel and body scrub. I picked out a clean T-shirt and a freshly laundered pair of soft shorts to sleep in.

Self-care, Sheenah, self-care.

After my ice-cold shower, where I managed to scrub the anxiety off to the best of my ability, I allowed myself to curl up on the couch and do some scrolling on my phone.

I tried not to spend too much time on social media these days. I had profiles, of course, but I was prone to getting lost in the abyss that was the *people you might know* sections. Inevitably someone would pop up that I knew but wished I didn't and then I would just spiral and be upset with myself about it for days.

It was better if I stayed away.

I opened my messaging app and pulled up Vivien's chat thread.

> `VIVI. Let me know when you can come model the Medusa.`

Her response was almost instantaneous.

> `OFC. I should be able to come home for turkey day. Is that soon enough?`

`It's perf. I'll just`
`need to steal you`
`for a few hours`
`that weekend.`

She sent me a string of emojis with heart eyes.

Anything for you, babes.

My heart lurched strangely in my chest.

I knew Vivien would do anything for me, if only she knew. It was so hard to keep my best friend in the dark about everything. I had stuck to my story for almost four years now and it felt too late to confess.

I was too worried about what she would think of me.

My rational brain knew she wouldn't judge me. I *knew* it. She'd be worried about me. Probably a touch upset that I had kept something so big from her for so long.

But my irrational, anxious, trauma-soaked brain was in control most of the time and that prevented me from finally telling her.

Things would be so much easier if I just *would*.

I chewed on my bottom lip.

`Are you going to`
`bring Tobias?`

I think so. Blushing emojis.

```
I haven't asked him
yet but things are good.
Am I going to have
to let my mom meet him??
```

I snorted. Vivien's issues with her mom rivaled my own, except I had gone no-contact. Throwing me out of the house had kind of been the straw that finally broke the camel's back.

I had seen nothing but happy, effervescent posts and pictures of Vivien and Tobias since they got back together after she almost fucked everything up.

From the outside, everything looked so perfect and happy and it kind of made me hate them both. Just a little.

```
Probably. But I get
to meet him first!
```

```
Obviously.
```

```
Can't wait!
```

I sent her a riot of excited stars and hearts that I didn't quite feel at the moment. I would get it together by Thanksgiving, though.

I would get my pictures of Vivien in my Medusa gown and then be ready to submit my application by January, or February at the very, very latest. GSAD accepted rolling admissions, but I didn't want to put it off any longer. I wanted to start in August...or the summer would be even better.

I was just about to put the phone down and crawl into bed when my Instagram notifications went off. I had a moment of panic—that Vivien may have posted another outfit of the day that I wasn't prepared for—but a quick glance at the account messaging me told me that the messages were coming from Sabbath Ink Studio and Gallery.

My heart fluttered for an entirely different reason.

Hi Sheenah!

Niyah here from Sabbath! We received your submission for the inaugural showcase at the gallery and would love to have you as one of the featured artists!

An email will follow shortly with additional details!

Peace,

Niyah

Office Manager, Sabbath Ink

My stomach churned with a mix of excitement and anticipatory trepidation.

Sabbath Ink Studio and Gallery was a new business in town. They had only been open a few months and Niyah had stopped by the cafe with cards advertising that they were looking for art for the gallery space of the tattoo shop.

The shop wasn't exactly downtown, but it had snagged a prime, scenic location on the road that led out to the nearest big city. So, it was a perfect location to attract visitors and locals alike. The building itself was a cute, squat gray unit with a black canopied awning and decent curb appeal, which was unusual in this town.

I managed to drive by it once, but was too nervous to go inside to scope the place out. I was afraid they'd take one look at my visibly un-inked body and ask me what the hell I thought I was doing there.

On a whim, I submitted a few of my paintings for their call for artists. They were kind of weird and I hadn't honestly thought that Sabbath would be interested. The show was on Halloween weekend and would officially celebrate the opening of the shop. The art also would allegedly, according to Niyah, hang in the gallery for at least a year. Maybe more if the artists and public really liked them.

Just be happy, just be happy, I chanted to myself.

The gallery show would be another talking point on my application for GSAD. The paintings were already done, so I didn't have to do anything there. But my mind was already churning, tallying up tasks I would have to do before Halloween in a couple weeks. Outfit. Business cards. Maybe I should take another look at the paintings? Just in case?

Thank you, Niyah! I responded, adding a smiling emoji just to be sure to convey my excitement.

Just be happy, I chided myself.

I went back to my text messages.

Oh, made it into
that tattoo shop
gallery, just FYI.

SHEE, THAT'S AWESOME.
You are so talented
and wonderful and pretty.

`What's pretty got to`
`do with my art? Lol`

`Nothing lol. Just wanted`
`  to remind you that`
`  you're pretty! It's my job!`

My thumbs danced over the keypad.

`I'm nervous`

It was as much as I dared to admit. And I tried to convey so much more through the phone, through those two little words.

Vivien took a little longer to respond this time. She was the wordsmith. I knew she was crafting something good for me, probably channeling her best advice columnist self.

`It's totally okay and normal to be ner-`
`vous, Shee! But you're a great artist. You`
`deserve this. You deserve this more than`
`anyone.` Then she sent a string of kissy face emojis. `Do you`
`want me to come down?`

My brain went almost immediately into denial mode. I didn't deserve this. There were people who worked harder than I did. People who were worse off than me. People who were more talented than me. There was always someone else. Then I finally processed her most recent text.

> Oh, no! It's too
> close to Thanksgiving.
> I know you're
> going to be busy.
> And have to bum a ride lol

Are you sure??
  I'm sure I could
  find someone going
  that way lol

> Don't worry about it!
> I'll invite some local
> friends. It won't be
> that big of a deal
> promise.

Make sure you send
  me pics of your outfits!

> Obviously.

CHAPTER THREE

STUDY OF THE MALE FIGURE

It took me several tries to get my outfit right for the Halloween gallery opening.

I wasn't usually so particular when it came to clothes. I liked to be comfortable and usually had a few staple items that I would return to again and again. I was the designer, not the model.

Eventually I settled on something that I felt was dressy enough for the occasion but also something that I was still comfortable in.

I chose a pair of dark wash flared jeans paired with a bustier-style crop top and a long slouchy knit cardigan that was another favorite of my shop. I added a plethora of rings and layered necklaces until I tinkled like a wind chime in a soft breeze. I added four-inch wedges just because. I didn't usually wear a ton of makeup, but I dabbed on a bit of highlighter and a metallic green lipstick for pizzazz. My hair was down my back in one long French braid.

I pulled the cardigan artfully off one shoulder to take a picture and sent it to Vivien for final approval.

STUNNING.

I felt good, but was still bolstered by her validation. Validation that I always found so hard to give myself after years and years of trying to be as small and invisible and submissive as possible.

I had invited Rayme, but they already had Halloween plans for the evening that I'm sure involved copious amounts of drinking and a skimpy Halloween costume. I didn't blame them.

I'd rather be partying with some drunk coeds too. An old high school friend had already invited me to a Halloween party she was hosting. I liked hanging out with her crowd well enough, but I had already declined due to the gallery opening.

I almost backed out at the last minute. I had the email all ready to send back to Niyah saying that I couldn't make it and hopefully asking if they'd still keep my paintings in the gallery.

Then I wrote the GSAD motto on my forearm with a Sharpie.

I could do this. I just had to keep my eyes on the prize.

If I could get to Georgia, I could go anywhere. It would have to be enough, for now.

So, I sucked it up, stuck my phone into the back pocket of my tight jeans, grabbed a handful of business cards, and headed out to Sabbath Ink Studio and Gallery for the eight o'clock gallery opening.

The Sabbath had its own parking lot, which was a blessing and a half. I didn't have the energy to get parking anxiety over my regular anxiety.

The front was decorated for the season, the door surrounded on both sides by towers of real pumpkins and hay bales. Black bats and witch hats were stuck to the glass on both windows; black and purple lights were strung over the double-doors. The aesthetic was very classy and witchy.

I got up to the door and I could hear the low rumble of voices and soft, ambient music.

I took a deep, bracing inhale before I walked through the doors. A bell tinkled overhead announcing my arrival.

Great.

I needn't have worried.

The place was absolutely packed and no one turned around to look my way.

I was frozen in place, a little lost on what I should be doing, bending my business cards absently in my hands, when Niyah, the office manager, popped up in front of me.

She was a petite Black woman with a curly fauxhawk and nails sharp enough to take out an eyeball. I would have been taller than her on a normal day, but I positively towered over her in my wedges.

"Sheenah, right?" Her voice was firm, authoritative. She didn't seem frazzled in the slightest by the crowd.

I nodded.

"I'll trade you." She held up a glass of bubbly punch, and held her hand out for my stack of business cards.

I switched gratefully. The drink would give me something to do with my hands.

"What...am I supposed to do?" I asked, eyeing the crowded space.

She waved towards the rest of the building. "Mingle. Network. We'll be introducing all the artists throughout the night."

I nodded again, clutching desperately to my glass of punch. Desperately wishing I had taken Vivien up on her offer to come down. She would have been totally in her element in the crowded room. She would have made me feel less alone and adrift.

The Sabbath was deceptively small from the outside. The inside was surprisingly sprawling, the ceilings high and airy.

The first part of the building was the tattoo shop and all related effects: front desk, waiting area, artists stations. A gangly white guy was currently giving a girl a butterfly tattoo on the inside of her forearm, the tattoo gun whirring softly as I passed.

The space in the back was the gallery, partitioned from the shop by a delicate archway and rustic beaded curtains.

There was a temporary bar, standing cocktail tables, a small stage with a mic, benches for sitting, and a *bunch* of people.

The press of bodies was making me feel claustrophobic.

I smiled at a couple people near the entrance and then squeezed off to the side, closer to the walls, turning my attention immediately to the art.

I took another deep breath, willing my pulse to stop racing, as if I could banish the anxiety by sheer will alone.

The walls of the gallery space in the back were lined with all different kinds of pieces—paintings, multimedia collages, and even some 3D installation pieces.

I walked slowly along the wall, glass to my lips, musing over some of the work.

I came to a very large, rectangular canvas, that may have been a good five feet across. The style of the painting was very high Renaissance, in the style of Titian or Botticelli.

The subject was a male figure, his back to the audience, lying supine on a bed of plush, vibrant blue and red fabrics. I couldn't really tell if it was a bed of sheets or a couch, but that didn't seem to be the purpose of the painting.

The purpose was *definitely* a highly detailed study of the male figure. His shoulders were broad, arms lined with thick muscle, the lines of his back carefully sculpted with brushstrokes, his waist was thick, not tapered, the round cheeks of his backside leading to thickly muscled thighs and calves.

I tilted my head in contemplation.

The pose of the figure was very reminiscent of the *Venus of Urbino* or the *Dresden Venus*, only we saw the back of the naked figure instead of the front.

"See something you like?" a familiar, raspy voice said from my elbow.

I startled, barely managing to keep my punch from sloshing, and took a step back.

Snake was there, grinning up at me since I was about four inches taller than him now. The vantage point should have made me feel powerful, but my heart was thudding wildly in my chest.

Snake didn't need the height anyway. Most guys got shifty when I towered over them; they didn't like the disadvantage. Snake was different. He was thick and stocky. He was a presence. He took up the space he occupied with Big Dick Energy.

I flushed at the thought.

He stood in his presence, again dressed all in black, the sleeves of his shirt rolled up to the elbow, exposing the taut muscles and tendons of his forearms. He crossed his arms, the position contemplative and not aggressive, and turned his body to the painting I was just staring at.

"So, what do you think?"

I turned back towards the painting. I guess there was no getting out of this interaction.

"It's...beautiful. There's something very...vulnerable about the position." I decided to test him. "It reminds me a bit of Titian's Venus."

He nodded, brows drawing together. "I can see that. I was going more for Ingres's *La Grande Odalisque*."

I nodded vigorously. "I can see that. But why would a man model himself off a famous painting of a concubine?"

I mused the question more to myself than to him, my Art History background swirling to the surface. I could feel the excitement stirring; the challenge of interpreting the artist's motivations and meaning.

And then it hit me. What Snake had said.

I was going more for Ingres's La Grande Odalisque.

This couldn't be happening.

I choked a bit, frantically scouring the edges of the painting for the label. And there it was, adhered to the wall at the bottom edge of the painting, under the figure's naked shoulder.

Self-Study #3
Figure in Repose
Snake O'Connell

I could feel the splotchy red crawl from my cheeks down my throat.

He had caught me staring intensely at his completely and utterly naked ass. Every ridge and curve and swath of skin painstakingly rendered.

To hide my embarrassment, I went for indignation instead. "*You* did this?"

He chuckled. "Why do you sound so surprised?"

I pieced together the evidence. His tattoos, the late-night working, the smudge of burnt umber across his cheek that night. Our worlds were colliding painfully.

"You're an artist?"

"Again with the surprise, Sheenah."

My head whipped towards him at the mention of my name. A name I hadn't given him. So how did he find out? Did he stalk me online? Ask another person in our building? Not that I knew anyone else or would expect them to know me.

Calm down, Sheenah. Looking someone up online could hardly be considered stalking these days. We were all online.

Still, my pulse rose and my heart hammered. He had found my name when I had already expressed that I didn't want him to have it. Any admiration I'd slowly been cultivating towards him—he was extremely talented, after all, I could give him that—abruptly vanished.

Something in my face must have changed, because his mild expression suddenly turned to concern, his smile turning down at the edges.

"Excuse me," I choked out, pushing past him, my arm brushing his shoulder.

"Sheenah, wait."

I saw his body move, as if he had reached out to grab my wrist, but changed his mind at the last minute. I'm not sure what I would have done if he had actually grabbed me.

I managed to keep my face carefully neutral as I quickly made my way back out of the shop. I did get one weird look from Niyah at the front door, but I just tipped my glass in her direction with a tight smile.

I wasn't *leaving*, leaving. I just needed to get some air, some space. If I was going to have a full-on breakdown, I would prefer to not also have an audience.

I slumped down in one of the wrought-iron black benches in front of the shop, abandoning my fluted glass on the sidewalk next to me.

I let out a breath.

The sun was just beginning to set, purples and pinks and oranges streaking through the sky.

I heard the door open and close and then Snake was next to me on the bench, his broad body taking up more room than it should have.

He didn't look at me, just slouched down slightly and pulled one leg up to rest an ankle on his knee. I got the distinct impression that he was attempting to appear non-threatening.

Way to go, Sheenah. Now he thinks you're unstable.

But I didn't care what Snake—this random man I had just met in passing exactly three times—thought of me.

I caught movement out of the corner of my eye. Snake had held up what looked like a postcard sized flyer.

"Your name is on the advertisement for the gallery." His voice was soft; I barely heard him over the thudding of my pulse in my ears.

The advertisement drifted closer to my direct line of sight; Snake's movements were slow, deliberate, as if I were a wild animal that spooked easily.

I took it from him.

It was a glossy advertisement of the gallery opening with all the pertinent details on the front and all the artists' names on the back.

My eyes scrolled down the back until I found what he was referring to.

Bryant West, 3D mixed media

Cara Reid, photography

Giavonna Oakley, photography

Haley Kinsey, 3D mixed media

Monica Stewart, fibers, mixed media

Sheenah Green-Barnes, oil painting

Snake O'Connell, oil painting

I handed it back to him, still without meeting his gaze. "How did you know it was me?"

I heard a soft chuff. "Well, I know everyone else so I just figured the one person I didn't know was you. I also may have asked Niyah when I saw you walk in."

"I'm sorry," I said. I felt the need to elaborate, to excuse my behavior, but I wasn't sure what to say to wrap it all up in a neat little package. Because it wasn't neat and it wasn't little.

"Don't worry about it. It's not the first time a girl has fled at the sight of my naked ass." He ran his palm down the thigh that was propped up on his leg. His voice was warm and light.

The tattoo on the back of his hand caught my eye. The ink was black and stark and looked fairly new. It was a beautiful woman's face with stone eyes and strands and strands of snakes for hair. Medusa. Interesting.

If I was one of those people who believed in signs or symbols or fate, I might be tempted to read more into this discovery.

But I wasn't one of those people.

"You mixed and matched styles, you know."

"I know. I'm a bit of a rebel, if you hadn't noticed."

"I think you're trying too hard," I said wryly.

His tattoos and black clothes and classic Converse were positively mainstream these days. But he laughed anyway, the sound deep and genuine.

"You're probably right." He straightened. "Look, I didn't mean to ruin your night. Can I get you more punch and introduce you around?"

A part of me wanted to say no and continue my flight all the way to my car and back to my apartment. Besides work and school, this was the most socializing I'd done in months. And I didn't really count work as being social. It was something I had to do, a necessity, and my customer service persona stepped in to shield me from the worst of it.

But Snake was being exceedingly magnanimous. It felt extremely rude to turn him down at this point.

And these were supposed to be my people. Other artists, my community, although I had never really found a spot where I felt like I fit in the local art scene.

I handed him my glass. "Am I going to have to see more portraits of your naked ass?"

He snorted, liquid brown eyes positively dancing with amusement. "Thankfully no. I only brought one of those."

Chapter Four

GIRLS WITH NO FACES

True to his word, Snake refilled my punch glass and towed me around the gallery introducing me to literally everyone.

The punch wasn't alcoholic, but it was bubbly and delicious and made me a little giddy—or that could have been the by-product of Snake introducing me to all his friends like I was some kind of famous person.

My cheeks were starting to ache from my smile.

He was so charming, so charismatic, it was hard for me not to be jealous of his easy way around a room.

Eventually we ended up working our way around the gallery, stopping every once in a while to discuss someone's piece.

We stopped in front of one of Giavonna's photographs, which just happened to be a series of dark outdoor photos. The lighting was dark and moody, so I couldn't make out if the subject was Giavonna or not. Looking at the whole collection, it looked like the models varied in size and shape, which was refreshing. Each photograph featured a scantily clad woman, either in the woods or in the water. At first, I thought the collection may have been boudoir photography, but the poses were not always flattering and not always sexy. Hair was undone, they were streaked in mud, gauzy fabric clung wetly to faces, breasts, and thighs.

I stopped in front of one portrait that was just the subject's upper body. She was rising from the water, fabric pulled tight over her face, ornate, gaudy necklace around her throat. Her head was tipped back.

"What do you think?"

I had almost forgotten that Snake was observing Giavonna's work with me. He leaned close to the portrait, hands clasped loosely around his back.

I read the placard next to the portrait. *The Rise of the Swamp Witch.*

"They're beautiful."

"And? You can't tell me that's all you have to say."

I pursed my lips. "They're subversive. She's dirtied up the female form, which is usually pretty and perfect. The swamp witch is about rejecting societal norms and expectations. They're rebellious."

They were wild, free, and unencumbered. They had claws and fangs. They had survived the darkness and were not afraid.

They cloaked themselves in non-conformity and danced on the shattered remains of expectations and should-haves and could-haves.

It must be nice to be a swamp witch.

Snake grinned at me. "So, definitely more than beautiful."

I found myself grinning right back at him, genuinely. "What, are you my art teacher now?"

"I'd give you a B plus for that analysis."

I scoffed, feeling like playing along, which was unusual. "That was definitely A level work, at least."

He cocked an eyebrow. "Let's see you try again."

He moved down to a new set of work, me eddying along in his wake.

I realized we had finally come to my section.

My paintings could be best described as surreal or abstract. There were melting girls, girls with flowers as faces, girls turning into birds or waves, girls growing feathers, girls with no faces at all.

I suddenly felt too hot, too vulnerable. To the general public, my work probably just looked a bit weird. To someone like Snake, a fellow artist, someone who studied art, someone as observant as him, my work would say something else entirely.

It became too much like a confession written in brushstrokes.

Snake had an intense, pensive look on his face, thick eyebrows drawn together. "Well, they are stunning, that's for sure."

My face flushed with pleasure at the compliment, but my skin still felt too tight over my bones. If we were to continue our little game, he'd ask for my analysis.

I was used to sharing my thought process about my work—a skill honed after years of art classes and artist statements, even a grant application or two. And then there was my application for GSAD, which was rife with self-analysis of my work.

But I had never been asked to explain these particular paintings before.

Before either of us could say anything else, a gangly white man sidled into our little bubble and clapped Snake good-naturedly on the boulder of his shoulder.

"Snake, my man, there you are." The man was tall and skinny, wearing tight jeans and an oversized T-shirt that fell almost to his knees. Almost every inch of exposed skin was covered in ink; he even had roses over both eyebrows. The man nodded briefly at me and then turned his full attention on Snake. "Can you take a client really quick? Nothing big, just a quick little banger."

Snake chuffed, but his mouth was turned down. "Really, man? I thought we were closed to the public."

The man looked shifty. "I'll owe you one. She saw your portfolio and really wants the pink triceratops."

"Oh, so this is getting you laid?" Snake raised his brows.

The man clapped Snake's shoulder again with a big grin on his face, as if Snake's cooperation was already guaranteed. "Thanks, man. I'll get your station ready."

Then he was gone again, melting back into the crowd from whence he came.

I swirled the dregs of my punch in my glass. "We. Who's we?"

Snake was grinning at me again. He did that a lot. "I may also work here." He thumbed toward the direction the gangly man had disappeared. "That's my boss, technically, but I'm here as a favor to him and I'm the best he's got so things are flexible."

An unexpected spark of disappointment threaded through me. Snake was going to leave me and then I'd be alone at this thing, *again*.

He sighed, shoulders flexing, the plain black shirt he wore hiding nothing. "Do you want to watch?"

"Oh. Would that be weird?"

"Nope."

And then he was moving and I was following behind again. We made our way back out to the front of the shop, where the stations were.

Snake's boss was standing next to one of the stations, his date already seated with her arm propped up on the padded table.

She was a leggy blonde, short hair slicked back behind her ears, chest and thighs spilling out of a slinky silver dress. I'd probably be making sure she got whatever she wanted too, if I were him.

She smiled as we approached.

"I can't thank you enough for agreeing to do this on such short notice!" she chirped. "I saw your portfolio and I just knew I had to have her."

By her, I assumed the girl was referring to the small pink and teal triceratops on the flash page that was already spread open on the table beside her.

Snake smiled his charming, perfect smile, without a hint of irritation. "Anything for my best man, Austin," he said in a tone that made it very clear he'd be calling in his favor. He tipped his chin towards me. "My friend is going to watch, if you don't mind."

"Oh, sure." The girl turned her sunshine gaze on me. "Are you next? I've heard Snake's the best around. Rumor has it he has the gentlest hands."

Austin snorted but turned it into a cough behind his fist. Snake readjusted his equipment and snapped on a pair of black latex gloves.

I flushed. I really did not need the image of Snake and his world-renowned gentle hands in my head. "Not today," I said instead. "Just here to watch."

"Are you part of the show?" Her full attention was now directed at me, unfazed as Snake shaved and prepped the underside of her forearm, right below the crook of her elbow.

I nodded. "I'm a painter and I design clothes and sometimes jewelry. Here." I dug a stray business card out of my back pocket and handed it to her.

"Really? Do you do custom pieces?" Her bright, bubbly voice had suddenly turned serious.

"I can customize most anything in my shop. And if you want something different that you don't see, let me know. I'm always up for a challenge."

I wasn't very good at selling myself in person, but the girl seemed genuinely interested, and I felt bolder with Snake there, for whatever that was worth.

She eyed me up and down, gaze critical and assessing. "Did you design your outfit?"

I twirled the arms of my cardigan for her. "Some of it." Under her gaze and over the steady buzzing of the tattoo gun, I picked out and explained all the handmade pieces of my outfit.

At the end of the forty-five-minute session, as Snake was wrapping up the girl's new tattoo, I had a custom order for a maxi skirt, crop top, one of my bangle sets, and a deposit notification on my phone.

The girl beamed as Austin threw his arm around her and shepherded her towards the door. I waved, feeling positively proud of myself for being able to promote my business like that on the fly.

Snake threw his gloves away and started tidying up his station. "I should have you around clients more often. She sat like a rock."

He eyed me up and down as he broke down his machine. The process must have been so rote to him by now, because he wasn't paying any attention to what his hands were doing. I was, however, the girl's comment about how gentle his hands were burned into my brain, probably forever.

We stood like that, just staring at each other, until it definitely got awkward.

He finally broke first. "Do you have any?"

"Any what?" My brain was fried.

"Any tattoos." His mouth smirked, like he knew exactly what I was so distracted by.

I shrugged. "Oh, no."

"Do you want any?" He was wrapping cords in neat spirals around his palms.

"Probably. I just haven't decided what I want first." I wasn't afraid it would hurt; I was just afraid I would hate what I picked and then it was stuck on my body forever. I was afraid I would pick the wrong thing, make the wrong decision, even from the list of options I was carefully curating.

Snake finished tidying his station and we moved to walk back towards the gallery.

"Which was your first?" I asked.

"This one." He turned his arm over to reveal a tiny wobbly black heart on the inside of his wrist. "I did it myself."

"Well, you've come a long way, then."

"I've had a lot of practice," he said.

He made a move like he was about to place his hand on the small of my back and lead me back into the gallery, but stopped short.

Did he see me flinch away from his hand?

I didn't have any time to find out because a high-pitched voice yelled "Snakey!" and threw her arms around Snake's neck.

He really did know everyone here.

He returned the girl's hug fondly and then gestured toward me. "Giavonna, this is Sheenah. We were just talking about your photographs."

Giavonna beamed, releasing Snake and turning towards me. She had long bright blue hair, matching eyebrows, thick eyeliner, and what appeared to be gold across her cheeks and nose.

"Sheenah? Sheenah of the flower girls?"

I nodded.

"Wow. I love them. We'll have to talk some more later. Snake? There's someone I *need* you to meet." She grabbed him by the wrist and he gave me an apologetic grin as she pulled him back into the gallery.

For a hot second, something like jealousy shot through my stomach. It was not a sensation I was used to feeling, especially when it came to attention from men. It probably wasn't jealousy. It was probably just some indigestion.

Why would I need to be jealous?

I finally had my chance to escape. I had stayed way longer than I had intended to, I had made some sales, and I had met some new people. Mission accomplished.

Putting my glass down on the front desk, I finally made the trek back to my car, feeling a bit lighter than I had when I arrived.

I was busy mentally patting myself on the back and fiddling with my car keys when I heard him behind me.

"Sheenah, wait!"

I stuck my key in the lock just as Snake came jogging up to me from the direction of the shop. The lock tended to stick, sometimes.

"Dammit," I muttered, turning the stupid thing fruitlessly.

"Sorry, Gia can be...gregarious." He rubbed a sheepish hand through his hair.

"No worries." I jiggled the key some more.

"Do you need help?"

"Nope."

He stood there, just in my periphery, watching me struggle with the lock to my own car.

Finally, the lock popped.

"Hey, I didn't mean to make you leave."

I pulled the door open on a creak, swinging my purse inside. "You didn't. I have to work early."

"You work early a lot," he said, like he didn't quite believe my, honestly, flimsy excuse.

"The glamorous life of a barista." He was still standing there so I finally faced him. "Is there something else you want?"

He grinned up at me. "Your number would be nice."

I blinked at him. "No, thank you, though." Even as I finally slipped into my car, I grimaced. Why in the world was I thanking him?

If Snake thought that was weird, he didn't show it. One glance in my rearview mirror and I saw him just standing there, waving at me, his face only slightly bemused.

Chapter Five

PHTHALO BLUE

I had told myself—too many times at this point for comfort—that I was not going to masturbate to the thought of my upstairs neighbor.

My body had other ideas, however. The tight, itchy feeling was still crawling through my skin, up and around my bones.

I could hear him puttering around upstairs, my ears weirdly attuned to the scuff of his footsteps or a chair leg. Or was it the leg of an easel? Was he barefoot and bare chested again, working on more naked portraits?

The fact that I had now seen him naked, and appreciated the view, did not help matters at all. I rolled around in my bed until the sheet was tangled in my legs.

I kicked it off in a huff.

Snake was infuriating. His cocky smile. His swagger. The way he filled a room. His apparently legendary gentle hands. There wasn't a single blown line or hint of redness on the girl's arm after he was finished with her.

It made me wonder what else he could do.

My hand brushed the exposed skin above the waistband of my shorts and I shivered. I was accustomed to dealing with my body's needs by myself. People didn't elicit such a physical response from me. Desire was clinical, a biological need.

Why do you feel the need to punish yourself? my therapist would ask.

I never had an answer for her.

Maybe I didn't need to.

I slipped my hand under my waistband, palm brushing my lower belly and then over the coarse hair of my mound. As a self-imposed celibate, I didn't bother with much landscaping.

I was surprised at the heat my fingers found. I took two fingers and rubbed them tentatively over my clit. The glide was smooth since I was already wet. I inhaled sharply and squeezed my thighs together, trapping my hand.

Was I really going to do this? Goose bumps rose up along my arms and legs, my fingers twitched, pressing hard into my clit.

I *was* going to do this, and I *was* going to do it hard. I pressed harder, rubbing the tight little bud with quick circles. Quick and dirty so I could finally get some sleep.

Harder I rubbed, until I could feel the pressure of an orgasm rising up through my body. I finished on a moan that was uncontrollable and louder than I was anticipating.

The faint rustling and footstep sounds upstairs abruptly ceased.

I snatched my hand out of my pants as if it had been bitten.

I could not have been that loud, right? He could not have heard that? I had never had a problem with the upstairs neighbor before—before Snake I couldn't even tell you who lived up there—but surely the walls could not be that thin.

There was a soft but rapid knock on the door.

I glanced at my phone: 2:10 a.m. The witching hour, apparently. The soft knock came again.

I got up and padded towards the door, flipping on the overhead light.

Snake was right there when I opened the door, leaning slightly forward so that our noses almost collided.

He was shirtless—again—that manic light in his eyes and various colors splotched across his face and collarbones.

"Did I wake you?" he rasped, with a small grin.

"Not this time."

"I'm out of blue."

My brain must have still been fuzzy from the orgasm, because he wasn't making a lick of sense. "Excuse me?"

"Phthalo blue, to be exact."

"Oh yeah...um...sure. I'll get it."

I didn't invite him in, so Snake lingered in the doorway, one shoulder braced against the jamb. I'm sure my apartment looked like barely controlled chaos to him. Clean. But barely controlled.

It was only as I walked away that I remembered that I was only wearing threadbare shorts and the same white tank top he'd seen me in last. It still wasn't cold enough to force me into anything warmer to sleep in.

The backs of my thighs burned with his gaze, but the feeling wasn't entirely unpleasant...or unwanted.

I rummaged around in a plastic box where I kept all my paint and picked out a few different brands for him. "Here, take what you like. I haven't replenished my supply in a while." I held up a few half-used tubes of Phthalo blue.

His gaze flicked briefly down before he pocketed all the tubes. "I'll bring some back."

I shrugged. "Don't worry about it."

He hummed, the sound deep in this throat. It did things to my body. My nipples tightened under the thin fabric of my shirt.

He was studying my face, eyes lingering on my lips, but also taking in my jawline, cheeks, ears, and the braids that hung over my shoulders.

I pressed my thighs together, hoping he didn't notice the movement or the slight closing of my knees.

"May I?" His gaze lingered on the edge of one of my braids.

I had my hair in braided pigtails. I saw a life hack on TikTok once that said that service people who wore pigtails got bigger tips. It unfortunately worked.

I nodded, my always-churning gerbil brain curiously quiet.

He reached out and fondled the end of one of my braids, the pad of his thumb running softly over the two-toned strands. His hand traveled up, fingers brushing over the shell of my ear, running down the side of my cheek and along my jaw.

His touch was featherlight, eyes heavy lidded and full of unmistakable heat. I couldn't tear my own away, watching him watch me.

"You have an interesting face." His voice was deep, dark, and lovely.

"Really?" In comparison, mine was a breathy whisper. I couldn't recall a time in my life that my voice had ever been breathy.

He was so close. I could feel the heat radiating from his body, sinking into mine. Something hard pressed into my back, and I realized that we had moved inside and I was pressed against the wall. There was no air between our bodies, chests pressed together, only my thin tank top separating us.

My hands shook with the urge to touch his bare abdomen. But I wasn't brave enough for that and they stayed glued to my sides.

Snake's thumb brushed across the underside of my bottom lip.

I could smell him.

It was subtle. A tantalizing, spicy tingle in my nose that I couldn't place. I inhaled. I couldn't breathe.

His nose brushed my cheek, hot breath licking down my throat. There was an answering throb between my legs.

His length pressed hot and hard against my stomach and that's when I panicked. It was swift and harsh and icy through my veins.

"Stop, Snake, please stop, stop."

The effect was immediate.

He stepped back, hands falling to his sides, his heated expression replaced with something else entirely.

Air flooded back between our bodies, sending goose bumps up my exposed arms and legs.

"Sheenah," he rumbled. "Are you okay?"

"No." I stumbled for the door; Snake retreated into the hallway as I approached. My hand shook as I grasped the handle in a vice grip. "I have to sleep. Keep the paint. Okay, good night."

And then I shut the door on his worried, downturned mouth, and pity-filled eyes.

I braced my hands on the back of the door, pressing as hard as I could as I hung my head and shoulders down. As if I could push him away even more by pressing hard on the door. As if I could push him any further away if I tried.

I couldn't stand the look in his eyes. The pity. I didn't need his pity. I didn't want his pity.

I was surviving. I may not have been thriving, but that depended on your definition of thriving. I was stringing life together paycheck to paycheck, commission to commission, shift to shift, but that season was almost over.

I just needed to get to Southern Georgia.

Snake was a distraction. I didn't need him or his hot hands or rock-hard stomach or enthralling smell or thoughtful commentary about art.

He was a distraction.

I had lost myself to a boy once before and I wouldn't make that mistake again.

Chapter Six

BLOW JOBS AND BUMS

It was really hard to convince myself Snake wasn't worth another minute of my time when my sleeping brain kept conjuring up different scenarios of what would have happened if I hadn't told him to stop in the doorway.

Hell, it wasn't even a *kiss*.

Our lips didn't even touch.

But that didn't seem to matter much.

It also didn't help that I found a stack of Phthalo blue paint tubes outside of my door the next morning with a note that read: *Here's my number in case you need any Cadmium yellow. Or anything else. S.*

His *S* was a huge, curlicue monstrosity. Finding the note had made me feel some sort of way I didn't feel like spending a bunch of time examining.

I added his number to my phone before I could spend time deliberating the intelligence of that choice.

I texted Vivien instead.

> I need Bryn.

Bryn was Vivien's advice column writing alter ego.

> *Puts on advice cap*
> what's up
> WAIT. PAUSE.
> Do you need relationship advice??
> My single Sheenah??

> ...maybe...

> CALL MEEE
> ANSWER THE PHONE
> SHEENAH MARIE.

Vivien's calls were insistent but I had to keep sending her to voicemail while I bit my lip to keep from grinning at her enthusiasm.

> I'm in public.
> I'll have to
> call you later

> WHATEVER.

Is there a boy???

There may beee

Omigawd
There hasn't been
anyone since Hunter
Right?

Right. Seeing Hunter's name on my phone left a sick roiling in my stomach. I tried to avoid any and all mentions of him.

But she was right. There hadn't been anyone since him.

In an effort to get back on track, I buried my phone in my bag and returned my attention to my textbook and notes.

Penn Warren University was a nicely appointed university, with one of the best libraries in the state.

The Penn Warren satellite campus had no such amenities. The satellite campus was a small collection of one-story buildings that were classrooms, a couple of shared adjunct offices, and one administration office. There were no study spaces, so I usually posted up at one of the tables in the coffee shop.

It was the most convenient location, especially before or after a shift. Hell, even if I wasn't on the schedule at all. It wasn't like any of my coworkers minded and I could still take advantage of my sweet forty-five percent employee discount.

Rayme was supposed to be meeting me, but they were almost an hour late.

I kept having to fight people to save a chair for them.

I tapped the end of my pen against my notes for Dr. Howard's third test of the semester. I was a horrible note-taker and usually did better when I worked with someone else. If Rayme didn't show up soon, I'd have to leave so that I wasn't late for my student-teacher conference with Howard. I wouldn't dare be late for that.

I also needed to talk to them about my upcoming shoot with Vivien and the Medusa. Rayme had been photographing my pieces for my admission portfolio. In return, they'd use the photographs for *their* portfolio.

It was the only way we could survive as creatives. You had to find someone who could do something for your business that you couldn't, and then you'd trade services. Quid pro quo.

I was just about to pull my phone back out to text them when the door burst open and Rayme came storming in like a short, nonbinary hurricane.

They plopped a wild stack of notebooks and textbooks on the table so hard my half-empty drink cup shivered.

I raised my eyebrows. "You okay, Ray?"

They huffed and finally took a seat, slouching and pulling up the sleeves of their flannel Henley. Rayme sighed so hard several people turned around to give us nasty looks.

"That bad, huh?"

Rayme buried their head in the stack of notebooks. "Coffee. I need coffee. It's too damn early."

"It's ten o'clock!"

They glared at me from under their forearm like Lucifer in *The Fallen Angel*.

I laughed. "Fine."

I got up and used my employee discount to get a refill on my refresher and get Rayme a very big, very hot, black coffee.

"Happy now?" I asked, as they took a cautious sip.

Rayme nodded. "You may speak now."

It was my turn to sigh, ruffling the edge of my notebook pages with my fingertips. "Are you going to pass this test?" Dr. Howard's tests weren't just like any old tests for any other class. We had to memorize biographical info, yes, but also works and titles and years and write multiple short essays. They were hell.

Rayme shrugged. They took another slow sip of coffee and fiddled with their lip ring. "I need a C on this test. And then if I get a B on the final paper, I'll be set for the class."

My heart sank just a little. Dr. Howard had emphasized again and again that he expected our final papers to read like we'd been working on them all semester. It was like he'd totally forgotten what it was like being a college student as soon as they handed him the diploma. He knew damn well none of us were spending the whole semester working on one assignment. He'd be lucky if any of us got started a week before it was due.

I stirred my drink. "My conference with him is later today."

"Oof. Maybe you can just beg him to pass you?"

I snorted. "If I cry, do you think he'll take pity on me?"

Rayme's eyebrows drew together in doubt. "Not in the slightest. He'd probably just take points off for trying."

That's what I was afraid of.

I definitely wasn't going to pass this class with flying colors. And since it was only a gen ed, I could technically still pass with a D. But if I could limp myself to a C, that would be best, so that it didn't ding my GPA so horrendously.

I flipped my textbook open. "We better get started, then."

Rayme chugged some more coffee, and then miraculously pulled out a stack of index cards from the mess they had put on the table. "I'll quiz you first."

Rayme started reading off questions, but trying to dreg up the correct answers were the furthest things from my thoughts right now.

This was why I had vowed not to get involved with anyone else. The absolute last thing I needed to be thinking about was Snake, but he was the first thing in my brain and on the tip of my tongue. I wanted to discuss this issue with someone so badly. I needed to expel it; rid myself of these thoughts via way of word vomit. I wouldn't be able to call Vivien until tonight and Rayme was just right there.

"Girl." Rayme's sharp-edged *girl* broke through my runaway train of thought.

I jolted slightly in my chair. "Sorry."

"You look literally a million miles away." They put down the stack of index cards, lacing their fingers together on top of them, like they were about to conduct an interview. "Now I'm interested."

I sighed again, throwing my head back. "There *may* be a boy."

"Boys are problematic."

"Don't I know it." I tapped the end of my pen rapidly against the table. Rayme didn't know very much of my past; not very many people did. We had a relationship built on proximity and mutual interests, and not shared history. We didn't know much about each other outside of our classes and creative pursuits. I didn't know how to tell them anything of significance without spilling a whole lot of gory personal details.

"I don't have time for boys," I said. That was a pretty good summary of the issue. I didn't have time to waste on romantic entanglements.

Rayme nodded. "I feel that. You like him?"

I shrugged, face flushing.

Rayme grinned. "Oh, it's horny pants feelings, then. Just bang and get it over with. That's what I do."

"Right." I sounded extremely skeptical. "That really works?"

"Sometimes. But sometimes the sex is really good and then you have to bang them a few more times just to be sure." They picked back up the stack of cards. "Now, where were we?"

The very idea of banging Snake not once, but more than once, had my body heating uncomfortably again, considering we were out in public.

That, of course, assumed Snake would also want to bang me more than once. I knew he wanted me; the *significant* boner he pressed against me assured me of that fact.

But what if that was all he wanted?

Did it matter?

No, because he was a distraction and I would not be distracted.

Dr. Howard held court in the temporary adjunct offices.

He was one of the regular instructors at the satellite campus, so he had taken the liberty to act like the shared office was mostly his.

It technically had room for four desks and computers, but Howard had one of the workspaces so decked out that he was spreading into the other stations with chairs and bookcases.

It was already dark this time of the year, but there were still other students wandering around the small campus.

I was early enough that I even had to wait in the hallway for him to finish his conference with the person before me.

The person before me—Brody—exited the office with a grimace. I unslouched myself from the wall and straightened the straps of my backpack.

"Beware," Brody said, "he's in a mood."

Oh, well that did not bode well for me.

I hitched on a smile as I entered the office and said a cheery, "Good evening, Dr. Howard!"

He was sitting behind the desk in full professor mode, with a tweed jacket and bow tie. "Ms. Green-Barnes." He looked at the watch on his wrist. "On time tonight, I see."

It was an effort to retain my cheery persona as I settled into one of the hard chairs in front of his desk. Maybe it was time to do some groveling.

"I really don't mean to be late, Dr. Howard. Sometimes my shift runs over at the coffee shop and I don't have anyone paying my rent except me. So, I need my job. But I really am enjoying your class!"

That may have been a *tad* too much because his eyes narrowed. "Ms. Green-Barnes, I'm not interested in the personal struggles of your life, just your performance in my course."

Oh, well then. Groveling was definitely not going to work. "They're connected, Dr. Howard," I pointed out, just in case he hadn't realized that.

He let out a sigh of the ever-suffering, fingers drumming impatiently across the desktop. "You're not special, Ms. Green-Barnes. Plenty of other students manage to balance outside responsibilities and show up to class on time and submit college level work." His voice was cool and aloof, his insistence on referring to me by my last name used as a barrier to keep me in my place.

I deflated. Of course, I knew I wasn't special. I wasn't asking for special treatment, just a little bit of grace every now and then. Was that too much to ask for?

"You don't think my work is college level?" I asked instead.

"Mediocre, at best," he said coldly.

His attitude just reinforced every bad thought I had about myself. That I was struggling more than most. That I was stupid. That I didn't deserve this. That I should have given up at seventeen and stayed knocked up and resigned myself to my fate.

"I'm an excellent student," I said in an effort to defend myself and not just roll over and accept his judgment. My hands fisted in my pants. I managed all As and an occasional B despite everything else.

He wasn't fazed. "I expect better than most."

I wanted to reach across the desk and strangle him. Instead, I just remained silent; I didn't have anything else to say to that.

I just sat there staring at him until the silence got awkward.

Dr. Howard finally cleared his throat and turned his attention to the computer screen. He tapped a few keys.

He cleared his throat again. "If you make As on both the final test and the final paper, you could possibly get a C in the course. Your attendance record is disappointing." He clicked around some more, but he wasn't telling me anything I didn't already know.

I hadn't actually missed any classes, but I guess he was deducting points for being late. I wanted to point that out to him, but his previous snarky comments had me cowed.

"Let's discuss your term paper." He steepled his fingers together in front of his face and wore an expression of extreme disappointment.

Here we go.

We were required to turn in rough drafts of our thesis statements and an outline of our paper. Naturally, I had thrown mine together at the last minute just to have something to turn in and not lose the points.

"I'm still working on refining my topic," I said, because I knew what was coming.

He nodded sagely. "I hope you are. Domesticity's impact on art is entirely too broad and is not a thesis statement. Your outline was also all over the place and barely cohesive."

I just nodded along.

"I'm trying to help you here, Ms. Green-Barnes, but there are no free passes in my class and mediocre work will earn the grade it deserves."

"I totally understand. I would *never* expect a grade I didn't earn."

By the look on his face, I don't think Dr. Howard picked up on my dripping sarcasm. Instead, he was just nodding.

"Good. I'm glad we're on the same page. I still expect a summary of your sources in two weeks. If you want to include a revised thesis statement, I'll review that again too."

I nodded my head. "Yes, I'll do that." I probably wasn't going to do that. My thesis statement was going to be a surprise for the final paper, probably. It was still a surprise for me too.

"Good night, Ms. Green-Barnes. I'll see you in class next week."

I gave him a thumbs-up and fled the office without a backward glance.

That was about as painful as I was expecting it to be, but at least it was over.

When I got home, I immediately went for the fuzzy socks, fuzzy blanket, and a bowl of popcorn for dinner. I curled up on my bed, popcorn bowl tucked between my legs, and pulled out my phone.

I owed Vivien a call.

It was late, but she answered with a squee.

"I can't believe you made me wait alllllll day," she whined.

I grinned. "Sorry. My day was completely packed."

"Understood. Hold on, let me get comfortable."

I heard some rustling, some mysterious thudding, and then a man's deep voice muttering in protest.

"Did you just kick Tobias out of bed?"

"Sure did. Okay, I'm ready. Lay it on me."

I grabbed a fistful of popcorn and stuffed it in my mouth while I thought about the best way to tell Vivien about what was going on with Snake.

What was going on with Snake? I didn't know, and that was part of the problem.

"Sheenah."

"Okay, okay. So, I think I've met someone."

There was silence on the other end. "You think? What does that even mean?"

I coughed around some popcorn. "I met my upstairs neighbor. He was at the gallery opening on Halloween. And then last night we kind of not-kissed in my apartment."

More silence.

"What does *that* even mean?"

"I mean"—I felt my face flush—"we had an encounter. Of a spicy nature."

I tried not to reminisce too much on how it felt to have his body pressed up against mine.

"Go on."

"I stopped it before it could go further. He gave me his number but I haven't texted him."

"So, what exactly is the issue?"

"I don't know."

"Girl, do you even read my column?" Vivien sounded a bit put out.

"Sometimes," I said sheepishly.

"If you want to text him, text him. If you want to have sex with him, feel free to bang him six ways to Sunday. Is that what you want?"

"I don't have time for a relationship, Vivi. If I get accepted to GSAD, I'm moving to Georgia, no questions asked."

I wouldn't give this town one backward glance as I hightailed it to Savannah, leaving everyone and everything behind.

There was another beat of silence.

"You don't have to be in a relationship."

I pulled on a loose thread on one of my socks. She, like Rayme, was suggesting a hookup, some casual sex to get rid of the urge. I didn't know if I could do casual sex; I had never tried.

"Vivien, there hasn't…been…anyone since him." I couldn't even bring myself to say his name aloud. "What if I'm not any good?"

That was another of my myriad issues. My body was reacting to Snake in a way I had never felt before and I didn't know what to do with it. Even if I wanted to have sex with him, what if I totally sucked at it?

"Practicing is half the fun, Shee," she teased. Then her tone grew serious. "Listen, you do what you want to do and you don't have to do anything else. You can tell him to stop if you're uncomfortable or change your mind."

Right.

I had told Hunter to stop and it hadn't mattered. The tears streaking down my face hadn't mattered. That was the first time. I might have cried other times as well, but I couldn't remember. Hunter had said it was okay because he loved me and we were going to get married and didn't have to wait anymore. He had whispered *I love you, I love you* against my hair as I cried.

It only took one therapy appointment for my therapist to tell me that I had in fact been sexually assaulted and it didn't matter that he was my boyfriend and it didn't matter that I had let him use me every time after that.

There hadn't been anyone since him. Almost four long years.

I felt the tightness in my chest; felt my breath start to be harder to pull.

Vivien didn't know all that, though.

I had tried to tell my mom once and she had scoffed and said that it surely didn't happen that way. And besides, Hunter was going to be my Godly husband.

"Shee? Did I lose you?" I heard her tapping on the screen. "Stupid phone."

I managed to choke out a strained laugh. "No, no. I was just thinking. Thanks for listening."

"Safe, sexy, and consensual," she chirped, quoting herself. "We're still on for Saturday after Thanksgiving, right?"

I let out a tight breath, grateful for the change in topic. "Yeah, I have Rayme booked for one o'clock. That's about as early as I could get them."

She chuckled. "That's about as early as you could get me."

"I'll text you the address." We didn't have official studio space, but I had managed to convince an old dance instructor to let me borrow her studio for a few hours. They were closed anyway for Thanksgiving weekend. "Thanks, Obi Wan, for your sage advice," I teased.

She laughed again. "Anytime, young Padawan. I'll send you over some pointers. Oh! Did you read my article about blow jobs?"

I snorted. "Yeah, I have it bookmarked for reference."

"I'm partial to number eight, when you sneak a finger up their little bums."

I heard Tobias rumble in the background again and Vivien said something that must have been muffled by a hand to her speaker.

It was my turn to laugh, genuinely this time.

I felt the budding tension ease from my limbs. "Vivi, that's entirely too much information."

"Sorry. I've got to go but text me updates, promise?"

"Of course. Talk later."

I heard an extremely girly giggle as she hung up the phone. I'm sure she did suddenly have to go if Tobias heard her talking about blow jobs and bums.

And, after all that, I still didn't know what I was going to do about my Snake problem.

Chapter Seven

DESPERATE HORNINESS

Showing up to Sabbath Ink completely unannounced was a bold move.

I still hadn't used his number that he left at my door and I hadn't seen him any more at our apartment. I caught glimpses of his tattooed neck and black jacket exiting the building, but he seemed to be carefully avoiding casually running into me.

He was respecting my space and my boundaries. Can't blame a man for actually listening.

It was almost nine at night, the sun had set behind the horizon line hours ago, and I walked up to the door of the shop almost hoping they were closed.

The last time I was here, I didn't pay any attention to the white lettering stamped on the glass. They were apparently open until midnight, seven days a week.

Lucky me.

My heart skipped a little in my chest.

The bell above the door tinkled merrily as it opened and closed behind me.

There was no one seated in the waiting area and no one manning the front desk, so I peeped around it.

The shop was moodily lit, with the soft sound of classical music drifting through speakers embedded in the ceiling. Just loud enough to catch the edge of your attention.

Three of the stations had artists and clients occupied, the whirring of machines and casual conversations bubbling up with the quiet music.

Snake was at his station, sketchbook propped on his crossed knee, his head bopping slightly to whatever was in his earbuds. He was wearing a tight, olive-green T-shirt, dark wash skinny jeans, and white Converse.

The muscles in his arms flexed with every move of his pencil.

He didn't seem to notice my entrance; none of them did, too busy with their own work on clients stretched in a variety of positions.

I scurried closer to Snake's station, wiping my suddenly moist palms on my thighs.

"Hey," I said, in a voice I hoped was loud enough to be heard over his earbuds.

His head snapped up immediately, almost comically. I might have laughed, if I wasn't so focused on not losing my nerve.

His face was surprised, but then his lips curved up in a slight smile, the hand that was drawing stilling on his sketchpad.

"Sheenah," he said by way of greeting, his raspy voice sending shivers down my exposed legs.

I had dressed for the occasion in an oversized crew neck sweater and tight bike shorts.

"I'd like a tattoo, please," I said, like I was ordering chicken nuggets.

His brows rose. "What are you looking to get?"

"A dress form."

"Where at?"

"The back of my thigh."

Something changed in his eyes when I said *thigh* and I had to resist the urge to clench my hands.

"Do you have a drawing or reference?"

I shook my head.

"Do you have a style in mind?"

Another shake. Shit. I had not thought this through enough. Dress form was at the top of my tattoo idea list. I had been with Vivien when she got one of her tattoos, so I wasn't completely oblivious to the whole process. But I felt like Snake was giving me the third degree in a way Vivien's artist had not. Or maybe Vivien was just way more prepared than I was and didn't show up to get inked on a nonsensical whim.

Snake chuckled. "A virgin, huh."

I almost choked.

I knew he was talking about tattoos. I *knew* it. But his liquid brown eyes were still smoldering in that strange way as they flicked up and down my body, searching for previous ink.

I felt a flush creep across my chest and was glad I had a sweater on.

"Yes," I managed firmly. "But I like color, and I'd like it to look kind of delicate."

Snake nodded like he knew what I was talking about. "Give me a minute to draw." He gestured back towards the waiting area. "I'll come get you when I'm ready."

My pride stung at him treating me just like any old regular customer, and judging by the little smirk that teased the corner of his mouth, he knew it too.

Whatever game I had started by showing up at the shop was afoot, and Snake was ready to play.

True to his word, Snake didn't make me wait long. I was barely seated in one of the bucket chairs, ready to scroll Instagram, before he came strolling up front with a single piece of paper dangling from his hand.

He held it out for my inspection.

There was the dress form, sketched in delicate lines, with a bust and hip line that was exceedingly more curvaceous than your average dress form. Wrapped around the form was a banner with the word HANDMADE inside; there were delicate flowers and filigree in the background.

"I won't have time for color tonight, but I can get the line work done."

I leaned forward, intent on the drawing. "It's really lovely. Perfect."

"Awesome. Let's get you comfortable and I'll get your stencil ready." Snake was still all brusque professionalism as I followed him back to his station.

He adjusted the table so that it was lying flat and gestured for me to lie down before he was off again to make the stencil.

I hiked up the right leg of my shorts and hopped up on the table, laying down on my front and trying to make myself as comfortable as possible.

Snake was back with a piece of semi-transparent thermal paper with my design all ready for transfer.

His eyes roamed from my head to the exposed length of my thigh. "I'm going to place the stencil and then we'll check the placement. Sounds good?"

I took a breath. "Sounds good."

He sat my stencil down and pulled on a pair of black latex gloves. "I'm going to prep the area first, okay?"

Again, I felt like he was treating me with kid gloves. Again, I couldn't really blame him. I was here to get a tattoo so I was prepared for the touching.

I pillowed my chin on my arms and tried to act totally normal. "Of course."

Snake ran a gloved hand down the back of my thigh and I tensed.

I heard him chuff. "I haven't even gotten the needle out yet."

He continued his prep; I caught the distinct sharp smell of rubbing alcohol, and then felt the cold press of it against my skin. Then it was the familiar glide of a razor. Then it was the slide of his palm again.

I tried to focus on the other clients in the room; I had a good view of the rest of the shop since my head was facing away from Snake's station. One woman was holding up a paperback in one hand while her artist worked on the opposite arm. I squinted trying to make out the title. There was a shirtless man chest on the cover so I knew it would be a good one.

Really, anything to distract me from the feel of Snake's hands on the back of my thigh, still totally professional.

I felt him pull the paper off.

"Let's take a look."

He'd taken his gloves off and grabbed a hand mirror instead. I got back off the table, Snake bracing my elbow with his free hand.

There was a floor-length mirror towards the back of the shop, so that's where we headed. Snake helped me position both mirrors so that I could see the stencil.

I contorted my body while he held the mirror and my arm, so that I could see the back of my thigh.

The stencil was positioned directly in the middle of my thigh; you couldn't see the curve of my butt and it didn't go into the back of my knee.

Snake leaned down, running a finger across the skin where the stencil ended. "I could go bigger, but if we go much further down into this area, you're really gonna feel it. Especially as a newbie."

I nodded, trying not to react to his nearness and the skin-on-skin contact. His tempered gloved touch was plenty. "Perfect. Very classy."

Snake helped me back to the table so I could get in position without rubbing the stencil off.

"Do you want a Squishmallow?"

At first, I thought I could not have heard him correctly. "A what?"

"Squishmallow." He dropped a purple cow Squishmallow by my head. "Clients seem to like them. Don't worry, I wash and swap them regularly."

I grabbed the Squishmallow, pushing it up under my chin and wrapping my arms around it. "Seems to be working. Okay, I'm ready."

Snake grinned, pulling on a pair of fresh gloves. "Let's get started then." His fingers slid over my skin again, this time rubbing Vaseline in small circles. "Just breathe and try to relax, okay? The first minute is usually the worst."

I took a deep breath and let it out again. I pushed my chin further into the Squishmallow, trying to achieve peak levels of comfort. Or as much as I could with Snake leaned over my ass with a headlamp on. His hand gripped the top of my thigh and my breath hitched.

Again, the chuckle. "Don't move. I like to keep my lines straight."

The sting of the first line pull shocked me into stillness.

I gave Snake about three minutes of silence—which felt more like an hour with the tattoo needle stinging across my skin.

I turned my head so I could watch him, adjusting the Squishmallow for maximum comfort. He was sitting down on a rolling stool, hunched over my leg. Every once in a while, he would pause and rub ointment over his line work, which was its own special kind of torture.

"So," I said. "Why only the outline today?"

He looked up, wiping down the lines. "Because this is a good four-hour piece and I'd like to go home sometime tonight."

I tried not to wince as he rubbed. "That's impressive, that you just know that."

"You have to. Time is money, after all."

"How long have you been doing this?"

"Legally? Since I was eighteen. But I gave my buddy a scratcher when I was sixteen."

"Austin?"

I saw him grin. "The very same."

"You're new around here, right?"

He rubbed again with the ointment, his fingers pressing a little deeper, maybe lingering a little longer—but I could be delirious from the pain. He paused and really looked at me this time, his head tipped down so the light didn't catch me in the eyes.

"You're chatty today."

I huffed out a laugh. "Just trying to distract myself from what you're doing to me."

He hummed in his throat, a husky sound that I couldn't tell was a confirmation or not.

"Do you not like when people talk?" I asked. I could shut up if needed; I didn't want him to do a shitty job on me.

He shrugged, going back to his work. "I don't mind. But, to answer your question, yes, I'm new here. I moved to help Austin with the shop."

"That was nice of you. To just pick up and leave."

"I can work anywhere."

That statement indicated a kind of nomadic life. One he could just pick up and leave. Was he not in school? I had pegged us at around the same age, but maybe he was older.

"Did you go to school?"

He laughed. "No, college girl."

"Rude."

"I didn't have time for school. I went right into my apprenticeship after high school."

"Is that normally how it works? This tattoo thing?"

He hit a particularly sensitive spot and I couldn't help but gasp. He immediately ran ointment over the spot, his fingers rubbing soothing circles.

"You good?"

We locked eyes as his hand continued to brush over my skin, and I didn't think I was imagining the heat in his gaze.

"Yeah, I am." My voice was quiet, but firm. I had picked the spot on the back of my thigh on purpose. The incessant rubbing of his fingers, the casual, unavoidable brush of his arm against my hip, was creating a reaction in my body. The spot between my legs throbbed in time with the throbbing of my thigh.

I wanted to press myself into the hard table to relieve some of the pressure, but Snake had said not to move.

That made it worse.

He cleared his throat, eyes back on his work. "No, that's not usually how it works but I am exceptionally talented."

I laughed. "You're exceptionally arrogant."

"It's not arrogance when it's true."

I could argue with him all I wanted, but I had already seen the evidence of his considerable talent.

I felt a surge of hot jealousy suddenly towards him—that he wasn't dealing with the bullshit I was dealing with school and Dr. Howard. He wasn't doing this song and dance to get to his final journey, he was already there, living and practicing his art.

I knew college was not for everyone—not in this economy—but it had been drilled in me as my only option. If I wanted to be an artist, I had to go to school first. There wasn't any other way, not if I wanted my parents' support, not if I wanted to make them proud.

And look how that had turned out.

Then, once I got started, it felt like a waste not to at least finish so that all my choices hadn't been for nothing.

I finally heard the consistent whir of the tattoo machine cease and tilted my head to look back at Snake again.

"We're done for tonight," he said lightly, putting his equipment down. He rubbed me down again, fingers brushing against the curve of my ass and the soft back of my knee. "I'm going to wrap you up then send you on your way."

The fact that my manufactured excuse to spend time with him was coming to a close sent a weird sensation through my belly.

I felt him put on the bandage and the tape.

I flailed around on the table, the paper covering crackling, before he grabbed my arms to settle me and help me slide off the table without bumping my fresh ink.

We ended up face to face again, noses almost touching.

It occurred to me that we were the only two people left in the shop. The other artists had finished with their clients for the night and they had gradually filtered out.

Snake still had a hold of my arms, his palms cradling my forearms. I could feel the heat from his hands even through my sweater.

The pain in my leg pulsed in time with my heartbeat.

The tension between us was palpable. I didn't know what to do with it.

So, I laughed. "Ow, it stings a bit."

The edges of his eyes crinkled as he smiled. "You sat like a champ, though."

I felt the heat flood my cheeks. If only he knew half of my thoughts while I sat there.

"Well, I heard you had the best hands." My voice came out lower and huskier than I think I intended.

Snake's liquid brown eyes darkened; they flicked down to my lips and back up again. I could feel the warmth from his breath.

"You didn't text me." His brow furrowed and his voice held a tinge of hurt.

It was the very last thing I expected him to say so I did the only thing I seemed capable of doing at the moment and laughed again.

I clamped a hand over my mouth. "I'm sorry! It's not that funny."

Instead of bringing my hand back down to my side like I should have, I placed it against his pectoral, where I knew there was an angel wing tattooed into his skin. I moved my hand down. The material of his shirt was thin, so I could feel the hard contours of his skin—his nipples and the planes of his abdomen.

He groaned, the sound deep in his throat. His head fell forward, until his forehead pressed into mine.

I kept going until I could slip my hand under the hem of his shirt, pads of my fingers skimming his bare flesh like I had wanted to do that night in my doorway.

"Jesus Christ," he ground out. "Are you trying to murder me?"

His skin was as soft as his body was hard, heat pulsing into my fingertips.

"I don't know," I whispered back. We were breathing each other's air, and the sensation was simultaneously stifling and exhilarating. I didn't know what to do with these feelings, with the practically desperate horniness, the neediness of my body.

From where my hand was splayed on his abdomen, I could feel the stuttering of his shallow breathing.

His hand skimmed down my side, grazed over the curve of my ass, and gently squeezed. He didn't move to press our bodies flush together, but his hand gripped me possessively.

It was a hold that should have sent my body into a panicked tailspin, but didn't.

Snake was something totally new and unexpected. I wanted to drown in him but was afraid of dying.

I wanted to kiss him—I desperately wanted him to kiss me—but I was afraid of that too, despite the urging of every nerve ending in my fevered body.

He seemed to sense my hesitation, my uncertainty, because he suddenly took a step back. Where his gaze before had been heated, it was now closed off.

Something squeezed in my chest.

I wanted to scream with the frustration of it all.

"It's late. You should get home." He rubbed a frustrated hand through the shaggy top of his hair. "And leave the bandage on for a couple hours, then wash it with an antibacterial soap."

I busied myself with rearranging my hiked up short leg, trying to hide my disappointment. "Oh, sure, yeah, it's late."

Lame. I was so lame.

"What else?"

He turned to his station and pulled out a small pamphlet, handing it to me. "Aftercare instructions." Then he turned away again, fiddling with his machine.

Well, I had been summarily dismissed.

CHAPTER EIGHT

SUCH A PRETTY MOUTH

I gave myself—and Snake—about another week of me dilly-dallying around and avoiding making a decision before I finally opened a new chat with his phone number.

Before I could convince myself to change my mind, I typed out a quick text.

*I think my
tattoo is infected.*

His response came almost immediately.

What?
Who is this?
Sheenah?

Yes.

I allowed myself to be bolstered by the fact that he guessed at me immediately, as if I was the only one he was waiting to hear from. I definitely probably would have died of humiliation if he had said someone else's name.

Come up.

I huffed out a breath, staring at those two little words. Checkmate. The ball was in my court.

I thumbed my phone closed, grabbed my keys, locked up, and headed up the stairs before my brain could catch up to my actions.

I didn't need gerbil brain weighing in on these decisions.

I knocked softly on the door, a small part of me hoping he didn't hear me because then I could hide behind the excuse that I had tried, after all.

Then the door swung open and Snake was there, motioning me inside his inner sanctum.

His apartment was the same size as mine, but whereas mine was crowded, his was very sparse. The kitchen area was spotless, not a bit of clutter in sight. The windows were covered with heavy black curtains and the bed with a black duvet.

There were canvasses everywhere, and where I only had one easel, Snake had several, all covered with work in varying stages of completion.

The only other piece of furniture was a farmhouse style bench in front of one of the canvases, with paints and palettes scattered haphazardly around on the floor. His lighting situation was interesting. He had some floor lamps, but had also strung some of those big outdoor lights across the expanse of the room.

Moody and cave-like were the descriptors that came to mind.

"I travel light," he said, bringing my attention back to him.

Snake had leaned one hip against the counter, arms crossed across his chest. He was fully dressed this time, but the Sabbath Ink tank he wore seemed designed to emphasize the spread of his biceps.

I shrugged, mouth suddenly dry. "I wasn't judging."

He tipped his chin towards me. "Well, let me see it."

I momentarily blanked before I remembered my manufactured excuse to see him. The tattoo. Obviously.

I had been meticulously following the aftercare instructions to the precise letter, no step forgotten. I had been exclusively wearing sweats or jumpsuits, because you weren't supposed to wear tight clothing. Wash, pat dry, let it breathe, non-scented lotion after day four.

I turned my body slightly, pulling up the hem of my loose athletic shorts.

Snake knelt down. I felt the soft touch of his fingertips lift my shorts a bit higher.

"Does it hurt?"

I shrugged, forgetting he couldn't see me. "Not really." The pain had faded to a dull ache—kind of like the throb after you got a shot—after a couple of days. "It's just a little itchy."

He made some kind of noncommittal noise. "Well, it's definitely not infected. It's barely even red. You've been taking good care of it."

He let go of my shorts and stood back up. "Do you want something to drink?"

I turned back around, adjusting my clothes—not that there was much adjusting to be done with my oversized tee and shorts—and Snake was holding the fridge open.

"I have, uh, water and exactly one Diet Coke."

I let out a small laugh. "I'm good, thanks. Thanks again for taking a look. I got a little paranoid there for a minute."

It was the flimsiest excuse I had ever heard and by the look on Snake's face, he thought so too. Thankfully, he didn't say anything about it, though.

"Do you have anything harder?" I asked, by way of segue. The thought of a little liquid courage was appealing. A little alcohol would smooth out the jittery edge of my nerves.

But Snake shook his head. "I don't drink."

"Oh."

"Doesn't fit my persona, does it?"

"Well, no."

He pulled the can of Diet Coke out of the fridge, popped the tab, and set it down on the counter in front of me.

"I never have. My dad's an alcoholic. I never started because I don't want to be like him. It was a chance I never wanted to take."

"Oh, I'm sorry, Snake." I took a few sips of the soda just to have something to do with my hands.

He pulled a tall plastic cup out of the sink and filled it with water. I caught the faint but distinctive scent of mineral spirits.

"It's fine."

His voice was tight in a way that let me know it was very much not fine, but I wasn't going to press him for any more additional details, the same way he didn't press me for additional details every time I flinched from his touch.

"Come paint with me," he said.

I was so taken aback by his request that I just followed him and his rinse cup to the bench set up in front of one of the canvases.

We sat down side by side and contemplated his work in progress.

Snake had only the outline of a woman's torso, starting at her sharp jaw and ending just at her navel. The outline was a soft brown and he had come back in with some green highlights.

"Are you stuck?" I asked.

"A little bit."

I tilted my head. The painting was a little directionless, the brushstrokes uncertain and hesitant across the canvas.

"May I?" I gestured to the haphazard spread of paints of palettes around the legs of the easel.

He hummed his assent.

I went to work mixing up a couple colors on a clean palette with a paint knife. I picked a couple different sized brushes, sticking one behind my ear and one between my teeth.

To get into the ideal position in front of the canvas, I had to step in front of Snake, which put my body between his knees.

He didn't move, but his legs widened slightly so that I could fit between them without touching.

I stared at the painting for a heartbeat longer. I had mixed up a nice lilac, a darker purple, and a bloody shade of crimson. I was going to fill the outline of the girl with flowers.

I picked up a glob of lilac with a flat head brush and pressed it to the canvas, skirting along the outline of the navel.

At first, I was able to ignore Snake's silent presence at my back and lose myself to the familiar rhythm of the brush. It had been so long since I had any time to paint anything, but it was just like riding a bike. My hand fell immediately back into a familiar rhythm; the scratch of the bristles and the smell of the paint were all familiar comforts.

I was totally lost in the experience until I started to become aware of the heat from Snake's body seeping into mine.

He hadn't moved, but I suddenly found my legs bumping his as I navigated the canvas.

I had to hone my focus, the movement of my brush no longer instinctual. I had to consciously ignore his silent body, ignore the way mine was slowly heating, ignore my breath and shaky lines.

My perfect, meticulous petals were becoming sloppy messes.

I inhaled and let out a slow, shaky breath.

I felt the slow brush of hot fingertips up the outside of my thigh. My breath stuttered and my painting hand shook, creating a crimson smear where it wasn't supposed to be.

"I can fix that," I whispered, eyes narrowing on my work.

He laughed, the sound low and deep and doing weird things to my insides. "Please do. I wouldn't want to see any sub-par work."

"I'll show you sub-par," I grumbled, only for him to chuckle again.

I forced myself to refocus, to feather out my errant red smear, to pointedly ignore the hot lines Snake's fingers were making on my thighs.

He was using both hands now, on both of my thighs, the movements infuriatingly soft and slow.

I had started this game by coming into the tattoo shop. And now he was raising the stakes.

I tried to get back into the creative zone, but it was impossible with the tight pressure building in my core.

His hand moved higher up my thigh until his fingers brushed against the inside seam of my shorts.

I gasped.

The palette and brush I was holding clattered to the floor, splashing paint on Snake's exposed feet and up my exposed legs.

I sagged into his touch, my back pressing against his torso. I could feel the heat from his mouth between my shoulder blades.

His hand kept moving up, brushing against my pussy, my lower belly, up my T-shirt, until his fingers finally touched the bare skin at the waistband of my shorts.

His hand felt huge against my stomach, his body heat searing right through me. If he pushed hard enough, I felt like I would certainly just melt into a puddle on the floor.

But he wasn't moving anymore. He'd gone completely still, even though my body was quivering with barely restrained need.

My breathing was raw and haggard in the silent room.

I felt his face move against my back.

"Do you want me to keep going?" His voice was strained, husky, thick like honey that sluiced down my skin.

Practicing is half the fun.

I decided to stop thinking and just feel. I nodded furiously.

"No," he rasped. "I need to hear you say it. Tell me what you want."

I grasped his arm with my hands, barely resisting the urge to push his hand down my pants.

He chuffed, low and deep in his throat. "Use your words, sweetheart."

What an infuriating asshole. Why was it so hard to tell him what I wanted him to do to me, to my body? Why did he have to wring the words from my mouth? The weird constriction in my chest was competing with the desperate throbbing of my core.

"I want you to touch me," I finally managed, voice strangled.

"Where?"

I was literally going to die.

"I want you to touch my pussy." I was so glad we weren't face to face so that he couldn't see the embarrassed flush that bloomed across my cheeks.

I didn't have time to unpack why that statement filled me with such cringe because Snake was tugging my shorts down my legs.

I kicked them off, not caring that they went flying across the apartment.

Snake tugged me fully into his lap, my legs dangling over his own. He spread his knees, taking mine with him, spreading me out obscenely to the room. One hand was bracing my thigh, while the other came around my chest.

I was only wearing a thin bralette under my tee, which was no match for the heat of his hand. My nipples pulled into tight peaks.

I wasn't sure what to do with my hands, so I used one to clasp the back of his neck and grabbed his arm with the other.

He chuffed against my ear, breath warm on my skin.

Then his fingers were moving again against my thigh.

They creeped ever closer to the very spot that I wanted them the most. He brushed against the soaked fabric of my underwear. I couldn't breathe.

His fingers slipped beneath the fabric, brushed against my folds, and I bucked in his grip. The arm across my chest held firm.

"Here?" His voice rasped against the outside of my ear.

Was he going to make me beg for it?

Did I care?

The thought brought surprising warmth to my belly.

"Yes," I whispered.

One of his fingers finally slid inside and rubbed quickly over my clit. I gasped, but the sensation was gone too fast, Snake sliding his finger down my core and lingering at my opening.

My hips bucked, seeking the delicious sensation again.

He rubbed me softly, too softly.

"Jesus fuck," I blurted.

He stuffed a thick finger inside, his way well-slicked, and I moaned.

"Such dirty words for such a pretty mouth," he crooned, his finger gently moving in and out of me.

God, were they always so chatty? I wouldn't know, I didn't have much to compare it to.

"If you don't make me come right fucking now I'm going to scream." It wasn't an idle threat; the sensations rippling through my taut body were on the verge of breaking me in two.

I felt the breath of his laugh against my neck. "As you demand."

And then he *really* got down to business.

His mouth latched on to my throat in a hot kiss, while his finger found my clit again, right where I wanted him the most.

His touch was firm this time, moving in rapid circles, almost in time with my ragged breathing. I clamped down hard on the back of his neck, pushing my pussy harder into his palm.

The orgasm tore through me fast and furious, wringing a strained cry from my throat.

My body loosened, but Snake wasn't done yet.

My body still throbbed and clenched, chest still heaved, but he thrust two fingers inside me this time and I could feel my pussy clench around him.

He went deep, pressing my body even tighter to him. "Go again," he said.

I almost uttered a denial, there was no way I'd be able to go again right after that orgasm. But my body would have made me a liar.

He crooked his fingers, rubbing against a hyper-sensitive spot inside me and I felt the pressure rise again, almost immediately.

I moaned. "Oh, God."

He nipped at the hot skin on my throat. "Not God, just me, Snake."

I could have laughed. I think I did, except another orgasm was tearing hotter through my body, so it came out more as a choked groan.

He held me tight to his body, fingers still inside me, feeling my walls clench around him, the feeling of being full and stretched extremely satisfying.

He held me until the throbbing stopped and I was limp against his chest.

I felt...light.

Satisfied.

He pulled his fingers from inside me, the wetness trailing up my stomach and across my hip. I could feel his hard erection pressed tight against the small of my back.

He brought his fingers to his lips and—as I watched with wide eyes—licked one of them from the base to the tip.

His dark eyes glittered in the low mood lighting.

"Good girl."

Chapter Nine
SMUTTY FANFICTION

Snake gave me a few minutes of reprieve so I could clean up in his small bathroom.

The bathroom was as sparse as the rest of his apartment. The pedestal sink contained only his toothbrush and a peek behind the shower curtain revealed a meager collection of body washes and soaps. At least there was more than just one three-in-one bottle. The shower curtain was black. Snake was ever on brand.

I was a mess.

My hair was mussed and flying free from its neat braid, color was high in my cheeks, eyes glazed, my underwear was uncomfortably cold and wet between my thighs.

I was having a hard time parsing out my feelings about what had just happened. I felt strangely calm, peaceful even, my body void of the nervous energy that seemed to roll through it all the time. I was also feeling sleepy, my limbs heavy and ready to curl up in bed.

Is that what good orgasms did to you?

I took a quick breath and straightened my hair up in the mirror.

Snake hadn't asked for me to reciprocate the favor. Would he be expecting that now? He certainly seemed more than willing, judging by the hard mass pressed against my back while I was in his lap.

Ugh. Why did this have to be so complicated?

I exited the bathroom, ready to do what needed to be done even though my eyelids were suddenly very, very heavy, but Snake wasn't waiting for me.

He was standing up in front of the canvas we had been working on, brush moving.

He had mixed up some zinnia orange that was a warm contrast to my cool purples. His strokes were bigger than mine, more sweeping, whereas mine were tight and controlled.

He rubbed his hand across his eyes, smearing the orange across his nose.

My heart stuttered recklessly.

Dammit, that was cute.

Two good orgasms later and now I thought Snake was cute. That was dangerous.

"She's almost done, don't you think?" I asked, since he hadn't noticed that I came back into the room.

He stepped back with a contemplative tilt to his mouth.

His mouth, that had been on my body but that I hadn't kissed yet. The skin on my throat seemed to vibrate with the memory.

I needed to skedaddle, stat.

"What should we name her? All good paintings need a name."

I shrugged. "Giving my work titles is the bane of my existence."

His brows furrowed. "'Girl made of flowers'?"

I laughed and he smiled. "No, that sucks. Let me think about it and I'll come up with something better."

"Sure," I said. I shifted nervously on my feet. "Listen, I need to get going. I've got an early morning tomorrow."

Then I realized I didn't know exactly where my shorts went when I flung them off with wanton abandon earlier. I did a cursory glance of the area but couldn't see them.

My face heated in mortification. Was I going to have to ask Snake to help me hunt down my shorts?

I heard his soft laugh.

"I think they're over there." His head tipped towards one of the other easels, where sure enough, my shorts were hanging off the edge of a canvas.

Face burning, I muttered a sheepish thanks as I went to retrieve them.

Snake had put his stuff down and met me at the door, stepping dangerously close to me so that I could feel the heat from his body.

It was an oddly comforting sensation.

His eyes caught mine and the intensity of his stare had me simultaneously fidgeting with nerves but also pressing my thighs together.

"Well, that was fun," I said, because I couldn't look at him any longer without breaking the intense stare.

Lame, Sheenah, lame.

He laughed, brown eyes lighting up with amusement. "I'm glad you thought so."

I resisted the urge to give him a thumbs-up as I opened the door.

"Sheenah," he rumbled.

I froze, his deep voice sending shivers down my arms. "Yeah?"

"Don't be a stranger. You don't have to pretend your tattoo is infected." His voice was warm with chiding amusement.

This time I really couldn't meet his eyes out of embarrassment for being caught, for being so painfully obvious.

I wasn't any good at this.

"Okay, sure," was the only thing I could think of to say before I scurried away back downstairs to my own apartment.

Vivien liked to send me links to smutty fanfiction starring her favorite couples from different books and movies.

Usually, I just perused them briefly, but I was five pages deep in a Brienne and Tormund fic on my lunch break.

I didn't watch *Game of Thrones* but I saw enough articles and memes on the internet to gather enough context to appreciate the ship that never was and why fans were so disappointed.

I was obsessed with the fic.

I tried to keep my face neutral while on break, but I'm sure my cheeks were flushing every time a turgid length made an appearance.

I needed it...for research.

I think I was drunk on the agency Snake had given me. I needed more ideas for *things* I'd like to try.

Brienne was a strong, independent woman who was struggling with enjoying the feelings Tormund inspired when he manhandled her.

I could relate.

I had to resist the urge to just copy/paste snippets of the fic and send them off to Snake. The only thing I had the courage to send him was a quick text asking if he worked tonight.

His response was almost immediate.

`I don't. Come up if you want.`

Again, with the ball being punted back to my court.

Come up if you want.

I want I want I want.

I wanted so many things, I wasn't even sure how to put them into words. I wanted the near-constant tingling in my lady bits to stop; I never wanted the tingling to stop. I wanted Snake to make it stop; I never wanted him to make it stop. I wanted his hands and his mouth and his body. I wanted to lose myself in him, so I didn't have to think about my shitty life or Dr. Howard's shitty class. I wanted to disappear completely in him, so I didn't have to feel the constant anxiety or the pull of the frenetic hustle culture that was barely keeping me afloat.

I didn't want to be able to feel the guilt anymore, the judgment, the insecurity in my choices.

The anger.

I was angry that I had let someone like Hunter steal so much of my time, my life, my agency. Even though I had finally walked away, the memory of him still haunted me, poisoned my decisions, poisoned all my other relationships before I even let them get started.

Not that I had a relationship with Snake.

That was getting ahead of myself.

Snake wasn't the only person I held at arm's length or pushed away. And I didn't want to do that forever. That felt like letting Hunter win. And I didn't want to let his last words to me come true.

No one will ever want you.

The words had hurt more than the slap across my face. The way he had spat them, lip curled, stuck in my chest and resonated harder than the sting of his palm.

I would succeed purely out of spite. Even if it killed me.

I thumbed to the next page of the fic, where Tormund had Brienne pressed up against the wall of the castle?—or a hut? The setting was very unclear—with his knee between her legs, kissing her roughly.

Thinking about kissing brought me back to the fact that Snake and I hadn't actually kissed yet. An oddity. Wasn't that supposed to come before the finger banging?

I crossed my legs under the table so I wouldn't squirm.

That was next on my list. Finally kiss Snake. Maybe while pressed up against a wall. Preferably.

"Well, isn't it my lucky day."

An entirely familiar and totally unwanted slick voice cut through my pleasant daydreams. My phone clattered to the table as dudebro Colton sat down in the empty seat across from me.

My phone had landed smutty fanfiction side up, so I snatched it back quickly. Before Colton could take notice of what was on the screen.

Not that he would notice very much of his surroundings anyway. He plopped nonchalantly in the chair like I wanted him there.

For our lunch breaks, staff members usually went somewhere else—ate in their cars, or used the smallest table, tucked in the back of the store next to the restrooms. It was a table rarely used by customers because of its size and inconvenient location. I'm not even sure how he spotted me back here.

He didn't even have a drink.

He was looking at me expectantly, I'm assuming to respond or say something but I was honestly just shocked into silence.

He raised his eyebrows.

What the fuck was he even doing here on the weekend? It was a fucking Saturday for Christ's sake.

"It's Saturday," I deadpanned.

His smile crinkled a bit around the edges. Was he really disappointed I wasn't jumping with joy at his unexpected arrival?

"What are you up to?"

I grabbed the detritus left by my lunch sandwich and coffee and crinkled it up in my palm. "I'm working."

My lunch time was over anyway. I got up from the table and moved to walk past Colton to get back behind the counter.

He grabbed my wrist as I moved past him.

I reacted purely on instinct.

My other hand came around and I punched him in the face.

I gasped in horror, dropping my trash, just as Colton hollered incoherently, hands coming up to protectively shield his face.

"What the fuck, man?" His voice was garbled by his hands, and maybe some blood. There was definitely a little bit of blood.

My hand stung. "Oh my God, I'm sorry."

There were not too many customers in the cafe, but a few people stopped what they were doing and stared at us.

Alanna came around the counter with a concerned look on her face. "Sheenah, what happened?"

"She broke my nose!" Colton howled.

My hands were just fluttering uselessly, as were my insides. I really hadn't meant to hit him; but I also hadn't been expecting him to touch me.

What would he do? What could he do?

My panicked gaze shot to Alanna. "I'm sorry. He grabbed me and I just..." I mimicked punching the air with my fist. Like she needed a demonstration.

Alanna's eyes widened, but she nodded. "I'll get the first aid kit."

"I need a fucking doctor."

Okay, now I thought he was being a bit dramatic. Colton bent forward.

I kept hovering, not sure what I was supposed to be doing. "I think you're supposed to apply pressure, not bend over," I said helpfully.

The glare Colton leveled at me over his hands would have withered my balls, if I had any.

Thankfully, Alanna showed back up with our first aid kit, not that I was sure first aid would do anything about a nosebleed.

She opened the kit and pulled out some gauze, holding it out to him. Colton took it, still glaring. There was a bit of blood on his fingers and some on his nose, but it wasn't spurting like Mt. Vesuvius or anything.

I had the strangest urge to laugh hysterically. I bit my lip to stop the laugh from bubbling up. I'm sure that wouldn't help my current situation.

Alanna bent over and examined his nose. "My brother broke his nose once. It doesn't look broken."

Colton turned his angry, righteous white man stare on her. "Are you a doctor?"

Her lips thinned. "No." She turned to me. "Sheenah, what about some ice?"

"I don't want her anywhere near me," he spat.

Alanna nodded at me. "I'll come with you."

We walked together to the stockroom, me with my rogue arms tucked tightly to my sides like a prisoner.

Our coworkers gave us curious looks, but everyone had otherwise resumed their business.

Once we were alone and mainly out of earshot, the panic surfaced. "Alanna, I'm so sorry. I really didn't mean it. Are you going to fire me?"

I felt the tightness behind my eyes, the threat of unshed tears. Now was not the time to lose it. I would beg her for my job if I had to. I couldn't deal with being fired right now.

I was wringing my apron in my hands until I noticed the quirk of Alanna's lips. She let out a huff of laughter. Was she laughing?

She scrubbed a hand across her face. "Sheenah. I-I have no words. I guess I don't have to tell you we don't hit customers."

Her words were admonishing but her tone was laced with amusement, as if she was barely controlling herself.

"It was an accident."

"Well, I'm not going to fire you."

I sagged with relief, grabbing one of the nearby shelves for support.

"I guess I have to report this to corporate? I don't really know. I don't think this is in the manager handbook." She was musing more to herself than to me and I allowed myself to breathe a sigh of relief. I still had my job...for now.

Alanna was still going. "I'll just comp him some free drinks and it'll probably be fine. How many? Like, six months' worth. Is that enough?"

I shook my head. How many free coffees was one bloody nose worth?

"Do you think he...will he...can he file a police report?" A new sense of dread sliced through my body.

Alanna turned her full attention back on me and cocked her head in disbelief. "You think he's going to file a police report when you have a corroborated history of unwanted attention and he touched you first? Girl, no. I'll go out there and soothe his wounded ego and assure him you're being disciplined." She added air quotes to "disciplined." Then she smiled. "I doubt he'll be bothering you anymore, though."

I let myself return her grin, even though I still felt shaky and unbalanced. My hands were trembling. "Do you think I could take a break? I know I'm supposed to come back from lunch, but, well." I held up one of my quivering hands and she huffed.

"Yeah, take a break. Let me clear him out."

She put her hands on my shoulders and gave me a weird little not-hug, before patting me on the back.

I could only manage to breathe a strangled, "Thank you."

CHAPTER TEN

USE YOUR WORDS

I managed to finish my shift without a further incident of physical altercation.

Drunk on agency, indeed.

A few good orgasms and I was sucker punching people in the nose.

Well, not all people. Just Colton, who had been making me feel uncomfortable at my place of work for months now.

And I deserved to feel comfortable at work.

If he was going to be butthurt about it, then so be it, and I would handle the consequences.

I felt much more confident about handling any potential consequences once I was removed from the situation, had treated myself to some ice cream on the way home, and was cozied up in my little apartment listening to the patter of a light autumn rain on the windows.

Much to my chagrin, I was eager to see Snake again and I felt rejuvenated and energized, even though just an hour ago I was bone-tired.

I dawdled, though, careful not to appear too eager.

I took a hot shower, to rinse away the smells of burnt coffee grounds and milk from my body and my hair. I took care of my tattoo with unscented moisturizer. I leaned in close to the mirror and tweezed away a few stray hairs from between my brows.

I fluffed my hair and ran a curling mousse through it with my fingers, then wrapped it up in a loose messy bun. I dabbed on brightening face cream and a smidge of mascara.

The weather still hadn't turned, so I put on a pair of loose linen pants and a tight long-sleeved shirt that rode my waistband.

Cute, but still comfortable, and still natural. It didn't look like I was trying too hard.

When I got to Snake's door, I could smell something delicious coming from the other side. I almost just wandered in without knocking, drawn by the delicious smell.

I knocked quickly and heard Snake's deep voice say "Come in" from the other side.

I didn't need to be told twice.

When I entered the apartment, I found Snake standing in the small kitchen, shirtless, in his customary gray sweats, with bright orange oven mitts on both hands.

He was holding them up in front of the oven in preparation.

I saw the timer on the stove ticking down the seconds.

That must be where the divine smell was coming from.

I laughed. "What are you doing?"

He shot me a grin. "Baking."

The timer dinged.

Snake pulled out two perfect loaves of golden-brown bread and set them on trivets on the counter.

"Oh, wow." I wandered over, entranced by the smell, to examine the breads.

"Banana bread, yum," he said, putting away his oven mitts. "Do you prefer icing or no icing?"

I pretended to think. "Icing, definitely."

He nodded, as if that was the only acceptable answer. I noticed he had what looked like flour streaked in his hair.

He grabbed a can of cream cheese icing and a butter knife; I leaned forward and brushed the flour out of his hair.

Instead of using the knife, he stuck a finger in the icing and then held it up in front of my mouth. His eyes were sparkling with the dare.

Without breaking eye contact, I took the lump of icing in my mouth, gently sucking down his index finger. He had been smiling, but his face darkened with desire as I cleaned him off.

"That's going to taste delicious on the banana bread," I chirped, and then flounced to the other side of the counter.

He haphazardly iced the two loaves, never taking his eyes off me, the too-hot bread melting the icing into puddles. His stare set my body aflame.

When he finished, the knife clattered to the countertop, unnoticed.

He came up behind me, body impossibly warm, pressing tight against my back. His erection pressed hot and hard against my ass and I had to suck in a gasp of breath.

His big hands skimmed up my sides, curling around to palm both my breasts. They fit perfectly into his hot palms and he caressed and teased my nipples into hard little peaks.

He nuzzled into my neck and slipped one hand down the front of my pants. His groan rumbled against my throat at the discovery that I hadn't bothered to put on underwear.

"Jesus, Sheenah."

I giggled. Like, actually giggled. It was a sound that I had never heard leave my mouth in my whole entire life. What had I become?

His wandering fingers brushed across my clit, sending zips of fire shooting through my belly.

The touches were barely touches; light caresses that did nothing other than build and flame the ache in my limbs.

They almost made me forget my mission. The kissing.

I wiggled around in his hold until I was fully turned around and we were nose to nose. A lot of girls wanted a guy who was taller than them. As an above average height girl I knew there were not going to be many guys who towered over me in that way. But I didn't see the appeal.

There was something extremely satisfying about being able to stand nose to nose with Snake and watch the slightly changing expressions that touched his eyes and the sides of his mouth.

There was also something extremely satisfying about being able to examine his lips at eye level. Snake's mouth was wide, his lips surprisingly thick, the upper lip only slightly thinner. A small shadow of stubble lined his cheeks.

He cracked a smile and I realized I had been just staring wistfully at his mouth for an awkward amount of time.

His hands roamed over my waist and cupped my ass, the heat from his hands searing through the thin fabric of my pants.

His skin was warm under my touch. I took some time to run my palms over his sculpted biceps and up over his hard shoulders and up the thick column of his throat. The hands on my ass tightened their grip under my exploration of his skin.

Our bodies pressed tighter together than I thought possible, his hot, hard erection pressed between us.

This close, in the dim lighting of his apartment, Snake's eyes looked almost black.

"Are you going to kiss me yet?" he rumbled.

I laughed. It was probably time to put us both out of our combined misery.

I slid my arms around his neck and leaned forward, pressing my mouth to his softly. I had intended to savor the moment, but Snake had other ideas.

His mouth was hot and insistent on mine, hungry and devouring.

Since we had put off the kissing for so long, I had almost feared that maybe Snake was a bad kisser, not that I had that much experience for comparison. Other than Hunter, there was only one other guy I had attempted to kiss and that hadn't gone so well. Granted, we had both been a bit sloppy drunk and the kiss had been sloppy and overly wet.

Snake kissed with precision and purpose, his tongue snaking out to tease my own.

Snake suddenly hoisted me up against his waist.

I broke the kiss to squeak and clutch my arms around his neck so he didn't drop me. "Oh, shit."

He laughed, his arms flexing tighter where they rested under my butt. "I won't drop you."

I wasn't a petite woman, and Snake didn't even start breathing hard as he carried me to the bed.

"You lift, bro?" I teased.

"Sometimes."

He braced himself with one knee on the bed, and laid us down gently. He kissed me quickly again, and then one of his hands captured both of my wrists, pressing my arms above my head so that I was stretched out underneath him. His knee pressed between my legs and I had to moan and arch against him.

He kissed fiery lines down my throat, his free hand slipping into my pants again. He rubbed my clit in that tantalizingly slow pattern that was teasing and not hard enough to get me to climax.

I pressed and wriggled against his hold on my arms, begging him silently to finish me off.

His nose nuzzled close to my ear, and his fingers kept up their slow tease. "Use your words, sweetheart."

Oh, fucking *hell.*

I pressed my breasts into his chest, trying to press my pussy further into his warm hand.

"Snake, please."

One of his fingers slipped down my center. "Please what?"

I strained against his hold on my arms. "Snake, please. Please make me come."

I heard his dark chuckle against my throat, but then I couldn't concentrate on anything outside of my body anymore. Snake set himself immediately to the task. His fingers picked up speed and pressure, while his mouth nibbled and sucked on the soft spot where my neck met my shoulder.

I came with a small cry, my back arching off the bed, legs shaking.

He pressed a quick kiss to my forehead and plopped down on the bed beside me.

I took a minute to just breathe and then I harnessed the feelings I had from earlier in the day. The feeling that I was in control, that I could take what I wanted.

I rolled over on top of Snake and straddled his hips. His eyes widened in surprise. I used my fingers to play with his nipples like he had done to me earlier. A lazy grin broke across his face and he brought his arms up and tucked them behind his head, like it wasn't affecting him at all, like this was just a walk in the park.

Challenge accepted.

Using my nails, I explored his chest, tracing the lines of his different tattoos. His chest and arms were covered, but his abdomen was curiously empty. Maybe it was still a work in progress.

He did have one small word across his ribs.

Trust.

I ran my finger over each of the letters, reveling in the twitch of his skin, the swelling of his cock between our bodies.

"Why trust?"

"Sometimes I just need a reminder."

I hummed, my hand moving lower and caressing the soft skin that covered the hard muscles of his stomach.

I felt his breathing stutter.

"A reminder of what?"

"To always trust myself."

My hand creeped lower, until I could finally run my palm along the hard length of him above his sweats.

Snake could no longer pretend that I wasn't affecting him. His breathing was ragged and his hips moved slightly under my body.

I rolled my hips experimentally. Even through both our pants, I could feel his hard length rub across the seam of my pussy.

He groaned, closing his eyes and throwing his head back into the pillows. "You're going to kill me."

I repeated the motion, his cock rubbing deliciously against my clit.

He gripped my hips, grinding up through the soft fabric of our pants. I leaned over him, bracing my hands on his hard chest.

He tugged at my shirt, pulling it up and over my head. His eyes were heavy lidded and cheeks flushed as he gazed at my naked torso, running his eyes over my small breasts. I flushed, and I knew the color traveled down my throat and across my chest.

His hand skimmed up my exposed sides and he palmed both breasts in his big hands, rolling my overly-sensitive nipples between his fingers. I whimpered, rocking my hips harder against his own.

My sex throbbed insistently and I wondered what it would feel like to sink down on the hard length pressed between our bodies.

Suddenly, Snake's hands splayed against my shoulder blades and he flipped our bodies and I landed on the mattress with a breathless thump.

His knees forced my legs wide and he settled his hips between them. Without much thought, my legs wrapped around his waist.

He brushed soft kisses along my jaw and his hand slipped down my pants, thumb rubbing over my clit in a way that made my back arch.

His warm breath fluttered against my ear. "Do you want me to get a condom?"

I didn't think anyone could make *condom* sound like a sexy word, but Snake's raspy voice did. My hips were grinding uselessly against his. I wondered what it would feel like to have him thrust inside me for the first time. I wanted him inside me. I wanted him to pound inside me, hard.

My heart started racing, stealing what little breath I had left. The hands I had curled around his biceps started shaking uncontrollably.

This couldn't be happening. Not here, not now. What the fuck was wrong with me?

I felt the cold sweat break out along my forehead.

Snake's eyes widened with concern. He sat up, pulling me with him. My body kept going with the forward momentum, until I was hanging between my knees, limp like a useless doll.

I heard Snake rustling around, and I heard him turn on the kitchen sink. Then I saw him sit down on the floor in front of me from my periphery.

His hand wrapped around my calf and it had an almost immediate grounding effect.

He held up a glass of water in my line of sight. "Here. Take a drink."

I grabbed for the water gratefully, spilling some over my hands, and almost chugged down the entire glass in one fell swoop. My throat was dry and constricted. I handed him the glass back, hand still trembling, but not as bad as it was before.

I noticed he had found and donned a gray Sabbath Ink branded hoodie. There went our sexy time. It really killed the mood when the girl you're getting ready to bang has a panic attack at the thought of your penis, I guessed.

"I'm sorry," I managed to croak. I couldn't look at him; I directed my gaze to his labyrinth of canvases and easels. I could feel the prickling of unshed tears behind my eyes and I blinked rapidly in a desperate bid to make them go away. "It's really not you."

"Do you want to talk about it?" He sat attentively at my feet, arms crossed around his folded-up knees.

Did I want to talk about it? I didn't think Snake was quite qualified enough to deal with my issues. I could barely deal with my issues.

Vivien always preached about open and honest communication in her column, but I'm pretty sure she meant more along the lines of "I'm dating two people" and not "I had a manipulative and abusive ex-boyfriend who got me pregnant, didn't want me to have an abortion, I did it anyway, and now I'm afraid to have sex" line.

Fear.

I'm pretty sure that's what triggered the panic attack.

Because I felt safe with Snake, I'm sure I did. I felt desire with Snake.

For years, I had myself convinced that what Hunter did to me wasn't that bad. Other people had it way worse. It wasn't violent. Just insidious, coercive. I wasn't ever allowed to say no. He would pout and cajole and accuse me of not loving him enough.

I'm not sure if Snake could handle all that.

I had been alone when I found out I was pregnant.

I had been alone, sobbing, when I canceled my housing at Penn Warren.

I had been alone when I got the abortion.

I had been alone when I told Hunter about it.

I had been alone when he slapped me across the face.

I had been alone when I cut off contact with my parents.

I would carry this alone, too.

"No," I said, and I was honestly surprised at the firmness of my voice.

The neutral expression on his face didn't change. He showed no reaction, made no attempt to change my mind.

"Do you want banana bread?"

The breath I didn't know I was holding left my lungs in a rush. "Yes."

He got up and went back to the kitchen, returning with two paper plates laden with large slices of banana bread.

He gave the biggest one to me and we sat and ate our pieces of banana bread in silence. Honestly, it was probably the most delicious piece of banana bread I'd ever eaten. I licked the tip of my finger and bopped it around my plate, picking up crumbs.

I heard a rumbling laugh from Snake. "You can have another piece, you know."

I smiled sheepishly and flushed. "Can I?"

He fetched me another large piece without complaint and brought a glass of milk over with it this time.

"I'm not a big milk drinker but I keep a half gallon on hand for banana bread emergencies."

"I love milk," I said, and then mentally chided myself because that was a stupid thing to say. It didn't stop me from taking the milk, though.

"Never been a fan."

"A lot of people say that, but I love it. There's just something about a really cold glass of milk that's satisfying. Sometimes, if I go a long time without it, I'll actually crave the taste."

And now I was nervous rambling. Snake didn't care about the milk. He didn't care about my opinion of milk.

I wasn't sure how to end this encounter with much of my dignity intact.

He'd shoved his hands into the pocket of his hoodie. "Do you want to go on a date?"

I almost dropped a bite of banana bread out of my mouth. "What?"

He grinned. "You know, a date. It's a thing people do when they're interested in each other."

"Oh. A date."

He wanted to go on a date after all that? After the meltdown and the milk tirade? Was he a glutton for punishment?

"Yes, a date."

"Okay, yeah, I can do that."

Snake produced his phone from somewhere in the depths of his hoodie and began flipping through what I assumed was his calendar. "I have to work late tomorrow, but what about the next day? What's your schedule like?"

Oh, so he wanted to nail down a date right here and now. Before I could make my escape and possibly blow him off via text later.

He was a sneaky one.

I felt my shoulders slump. "Oh, uh, I'm closing so I won't get off till seven."

"Great. I can pick you up at eight-thirty. Does that work?"

Well, I guessed it did.

Chapter Eleven

GIRL WORTH KNOWING

Going on an actual date with Snake was not part of my master plan to not make him a distraction. This was just supposed to be for fun.

The more time I spent with him just made me like him a bit more.

And liking him wasn't part of the plan.

That was veering into very dangerous territory.

One date won't hurt, I tried to convince myself. One date did not a relationship make. I could handle one date.

I was able to cut out of work a few minutes early, so I could get home, get showered, and get ready with a few minutes to spare.

Snake said we were going to throw axes and that I had to wear closed-toe shoes, which kind of limited my outfit choices. Not that I was trying to impress him with my clothes, anyway.

In the end, I decided to go super casual in a pair of black leggings, oversized plain white tee, a cropped jean jacket, and a chunky knit scarf from my shop. I was a little heavier handed with the eyeliner, and spent more time than necessary straightening out my two-toned bangs so they laid airy and effortless against my forehead.

Not trying to impress him at all. Not me.

At exactly eight-thirty there was a quick rap on my front door.

I knew as soon as I opened the door that this date was going to be a huge mistake.

Snake looked *hot*.

Ugh, so hot.

He was wearing a pair of ridiculously tight black skinny jeans with artistic rips across both thighs, an oatmeal colored, tailored hoodie, and oatmeal-colored high-top sneakers from a brand I didn't recognize.

And he smelled *divine*.

His signature smokey, spicy scent tickled my nose as I stepped out into the hallway.

"Hi," he said, with a grin.

"Are you going to be able to move in those?" I raised my eyebrows at his tight pants.

He chuckled. It was a sound that rumbled deep in his chest and caused my stomach to lurch in response.

"Don't you worry about the way I move," he said, sticking his elbow out towards me.

What? Was I supposed to take his arm? Were we going for a stroll around the promenade?

I stuck my hand into the crook of his elbow anyway. Promenade away.

Snake tucked my hand tighter, my body bumping into his, his warmth seeping into my bones. I had to resist the urge to sigh.

"Just to let you know, I'm not very competitive," I said.

That was a lie. I was extremely competitive when it came to games. It was a huge flaw. I had caused many a hurt feeling at sleepovers. One girl stopped talking to me over a particularly vicious game of Monopoly.

I would crush him.

The ride over to The Axe House was only about twenty-five minutes and I didn't have to worry about it being awkward because Snake was more than willing to fill the silence with client horror stories. I hadn't realized tattoo shops were filled with more drama than a reality TV show.

Snake's car was surprisingly nice but most things were nice compared to my beat-up old ride. His midsize SUV had heated leather seats that felt like velvet under my fingers. I turned the heat up on mine so my butt was toasty warm. It was also spotless. Like, not a stray napkin or straw wrapper or discarded coffee cup anywhere. It smelled like him.

The Axe House was located in the hippy part of town, which made sense, as I assumed that was their target audience.

Snake held the door for me as we entered, his hand brushing the small of my back.

We were immediately greeted by a white guy with short cropped hair in a red T-shirt with COACH emblazoned across his chest. Tattoo sleeves peeked out from his shirt.

"Snake, my man," he greeted, fist-bumping my date.

I raised my eyebrows. "You come here often?"

"I'm in the league." He gave me a shit-eating grin.

The coach said, "He's one of our best guys."

I think my mouth might have dropped open because Snake elbowed me in the side. "Not that competitive, huh?"

What a sneaky bastard. "Get ready to eat my steel." Were axes made of steel? I had no idea but it sounded good and made Snake chuckle, his eyes lighting up.

We started following the coach guy to our lane and associated table, when Snake leaned over and whispered in my ear, "I'll eat anything you want."

His silky voice caused me to trip over my booties.

Snake grabbed my elbow, liquid brown eyes dancing in amusement. Neither of us were really listening to the instructions coach guy was imparting, but I guessed since Snake was *part of the league*, I didn't need to pay much attention.

"I'll get y'all some drinks."

I gave Snake a startled look. "You can drink here? With the weapons?"

He shrugged out of his hoodie—shirt hem riding up to expose the tempting flesh above his waistband—and laid it over one of the high chairs.

"You can drink, but you can't get drunk. They cut you off. Because of the weapons."

Well, that made perfect sense. It also seemed like the perfect place for someone like him, who wasn't a drinker. So much of drinking culture was socialization, so I imagined it would be hard for him to surround himself with people who were drinking to excess.

"Does it bother you?"

He had on a tight T-shirt under his hoodie, one that strained against his arms and chest, which was terribly distracting. "Does what bother me?" Now he was doing some weird stretching with his arms, which made the muscle bulging even worse.

I pulled off my jacket, hanging it on the back of my chair. "When people drink around you."

He pulled one of his arms across his chest with the other, in what I assume was another stretch. I mimicked his motions, even though I was pretty sure they were not going to do me any good.

"Not really." He paused, brows creasing. "It's hard to avoid at my age. There aren't many twenty-three-year-olds who've already given up alcohol." Then he shrugged. "I try to just not put myself in those situations. I'm sure it's a great time, but..." he trailed off.

Snake's voice had gone low and his expression serious, for all the bantering we were doing not moments earlier. I had a feeling we had wandered into sensitive territory for him, and I wanted to respect his boundaries the way he had been respecting mine.

But what lingered on the edge of my tongue, but I was too much of a chicken to prompt him further and Coach had chosen that time to reappear with a metal bucket full of ice and a variety of longneck bottles.

I glanced at the IPAs. "Oh, hipster beer!"

Then I winced. *Way to change the subject, Sheenah.*

But he just smiled and shook his head, like he was accustomed to my tomfoolery. "Do you know how to play?"

I twisted the top off one of the IPAs. I wasn't really a beer person, but I figured it couldn't make my aim any worse. "Nope."

"Well, the rules of the game are simple." He gestured down our lane towards the target at the end. The area was arranged kind of like a bowling alley, except instead of pins at the end, you had well-worn targets.

Each party had their own lane and cocktail table like ours and people took turns throwing their axes, while the others drank and watched and laughed if an axe thunked against the target and went flying towards the barriers.

"We'll play three rounds and highest total score wins. You'll get five throws per round. You score points for each axe that sticks to the target. The bull's-eye is five points, the small circle is three, and the outer rim is worth one." He was gesturing to the target, pointing out the different places on the target my axe could land, but I was too distracted by his arms and the fact that he'd said rim.

Yes, this date was a horrible idea.

"Sheenah."

Oops.

"Yeah, easy-peasy. Hit the target with the axe. Got it." I gave him a thumbs-up as I took a quick swig of the beer and tried not to pull a face. Hoppy beer was not my thing.

"Do you want to take a few practice shots?"

I shrugged. "Sure."

I joined Snake at the end of our lane, where our axes were stuck into the wood.

"Show me your stance."

I yanked one of the axes out of the wood, planted my feet, and held the handle of the axe like I would a baseball bat.

"Well, that looks awful."

I almost laughed at the disappointed look on Snake's face.

"Absolutely not," he said, coming up to stand behind me. His hands were light on my arms and waist as I allowed him to reposition my upper body. The only thing I could do was grin at the target.

He worked on my hands next, his warm skin sliding over mine. "You want a lighter grip." He adjusted the handle in my palm. "A light grip will let the axe almost release itself."

His fingers were sliding through mine, loosening my grip on the handle to the desired strength. His body was pressed flush against my back; I could feel the rise and fall of his chest.

"Feel that?" he asked.

"I feel something," I said, wiggling my hips slightly.

His breathing hitched, his fingers flexing reflexively over mine.

"You're messing up my grip," I chided.

He laughed, breath skimming over my throat. "Let's see what you've got, then."

Snake finally stepped back, crossing his arms over his chest as he observed.

I inhaled a quick breath to center my body, released the tension in my shoulders, took a small step forward, and let my axe fly.

It thunked cleanly into the red bull's-eye.

I flipped my hair and looked back over my shoulder at Snake, whose mouth was slightly agape.

"That's five points, right?"

He gaped for a few more seconds and then stalked up to the lane and grabbed his own axe. "That's enough practice. Let's go."

Watching Snake throw axes was a transformative, erotic experience. His body was graceful, but moved with power and precision, as each of his throws sunk cleanly in the bull's-eye.

My first shot had been a lucky throw. The taunting of Snake had been satisfying, but it was still a lucky throw nonetheless. I'm not sure I'd be able to repeat the performance, but maybe Snake could correct my grip again.

The thought of him rubbing up against my back again made me all warm inside.

Snake finished his turn, puffed his chest, and flexed his arms. "That's twenty-five points for me, right?"

I took a swig of my drink. "Yeah, yeah, yeah."

I let him gloat and flex because he was just too cute. I shimmied past him to grab an axe and his hands casually brushed against my hips and waist.

I picked up an axe, purposely misadjusting my grip in the hopes of tempting Snake to come fix it.

I heard his soft chuckle behind me and grinned to myself.

But then I heard something above Snake's laugh—something brash and loud and all too familiar. The sound made my blood run cold and my skin crawl.

This could not be happening to me. Right now.

The axe slipped from my numb fingers; I barely heard it clatter to the floor. I was probably lucky it didn't land on my foot.

I couldn't draw breath.

My head whipped around, eyes frantically scanning the crowd. I didn't notice anything unusual or noteworthy when we came in.

Finally, I spotted him, several lanes down, in the middle of a crowd of people.

He was still tall, his floppy blond hair sticking out over the heads of the other people. He used to be gangly, but now I guessed it could be described as lean. His shoulders had filled out. He was laughing and smiling and my stomach roiled with barely contained nausea.

He wasn't supposed to be here. I wasn't ever supposed to see him again.

He was supposed to be three states away, attending school at his fancy, expensive, private college. He hadn't been forced to give up his scholarship or his dorm. He hadn't been forced to change the entire trajectory of his life.

He'd been able to continue with his plans, continue on to his fancy college without a backward glance.

That's what happened to boys who ruined girls.

They continued on with their lives as if nothing had happened, leaving the scraps and shards of broken girls in their wake.

I think my whole body may have been vibrating with barely suppressed rage.

He was supposed to have *left*.

"Sheenah."

Snake's insistent voice finally broke through my rapidly churning thoughts. I couldn't seem to focus on his face, but the tone of his voice made it seem like it wasn't the first time he'd said my name.

Suddenly, my world tilted completely on its axis, the interior of the The Axe House slanting at a weird angle.

It took me several seconds to realize Snake had bodily picked me up in a princess carry, arms braced behind my knees and shoulders.

I squeaked and wrapped my hands around his neck. We were the same damn height, for fuck's sake.

If my weight bothered Snake, he didn't let it show. He just hefted me closer to his chest and I rested my chin on his shoulder, watching Hunter's profile disappear as we left.

If anyone thought it was weird that Snake abruptly carried me out, they didn't say anything.

Snake carried me to the passenger side of his car and handed me my jacket and scarf, still without speaking.

The drive back to our apartment complex was quiet. I didn't know what to say so I just stared out the window and nibbled at the skin around my fingernails.

Snake pulled into a parking spot, cut the engine, and took his seat belt off, but didn't speak or make any other moves to get out of the car.

His hands gripped the steering wheel until his knuckles were white.

"Did he hurt you?"

His question was quiet, but I still felt its echo in the confined space of the front seat. I rubbed my palms on my thighs.

"Yes," I said, simply. Because it was true. And because I was tired of carrying it.

He released the steering wheel with an exhale of breath, as if it was the hardest thing he'd ever done.

"My dad...hits my mom...when he's drunk. And he's always drunk." His fingers flexed again on the wheel. "That's why I don't drink. I don't want to be anything like him. That's why I don't go home."

My heart cracked in my chest, for Snake the man who couldn't go home, who was haunted by the sins of his father. And Snake the little boy, who must have grown up watching the father he admired abuse the mother he adored.

"Did he hit you?"

Snake shook his head. "He took a swing once, and then I took a swing back with my baseball bat. I was twelve. And it still wasn't enough to make her leave."

I wanted to tell him it obviously wasn't his fault. He was the child; they were the adults. But that line usually didn't change anything.

I had been told it wasn't my fault too, and it changed very little.

It didn't change the fact that it happened, that we had to live with the repercussions. It didn't change the fact that my whole body trembled when I heard his laugh.

I leaned over and ran my fingers through the soft hair on the top of Snake's head, trailed them through the shorter hair down the back, and ran them across the nape of his neck. I squeezed gently, just so he would know he wasn't alone.

He let out a breath, lashes fluttering momentarily, fingers losing their vice-grip on the steering wheel.

"It was only once," I confessed. "He only hit me once."

"That's not all," he said, and it wasn't phrased like a question.

"No, that's not all."

I wondered if I had the courage to say it out loud to him, something I hadn't even had the courage to tell my best friend in the whole world.

I had told my mom, once, and I had told my therapist, but she was getting paid to deal with my trauma. I trusted that she could handle it, since she was a professional, after all.

My hand tightened on his neck.

I wasn't sure what to say that wouldn't make him run the other direction. How could I succinctly summarize almost four years of my life?

I didn't want to be damaged goods. I didn't want Snake to think I wasn't worth his time.

And *rape* still felt too serious. Rape brought back my mom's words. *Hunter wouldn't do something like that. He's a nice boy. He goes to church. You didn't fight. You didn't go to the police. You didn't even break up with him. What kind of girl does that? What kind of victim?*

"Listen, it's okay if you don't want to tell me. You don't—"

"He sexually assaulted me." The words came out in one breathless rush. The words blurred into each other, and I barely understood them, so I would be surprised if Snake could. Except, his shoulders tensed and his body stilled.

I pushed on, focusing on a nonexistent dust bunny on the black dash. "No-not every time, but enough."

But enough. What kind of explanation is that, Sheenah?

I leaned further over the middle console, pressing my nose into his throat. My free hand slid up his thigh. He wasn't hard, but I could still feel him through his tight jeans.

He inhaled sharply. "Sheenah, you don't—"

I pressed my mouth to his pulse, which was fluttering rapidly. "Please. I want to. I need to. I need..." I struggled to find a word to accurately describe my feeling, my need. I wanted to disappear, I wanted to forget, I didn't want Hunter's hands to be the only memory on my skin.

I wanted to be...normal. I think that was the crux of the issue. I wanted to be a normal person having normal sex. I was supposed to be normal. I was supposed to be living a normal life as a normal college student. Not dealing with this shit.

But Snake was finally taking his keys out of the ignition and coming around to the passenger door. He took my hand like he was helping me out of a carriage in a period drama.

His hand never let mine go as we walked into the apartment complex and up the stairs to his apartment.

As always, his place was tidy and airy and I felt like I could breathe. His blackout curtains were open for once, so I could see the downtown city lights on the horizon.

We lay down on the bed together, still fully clothed, and for a while just breathed.

Snake had his head on my chest and my arms were laced around his broad shoulders. One of his legs was thrown over mine.

The weight of his body and steadiness of his breathing was comforting, grounding.

After a few minutes of calm breathing, the energy in the room changed. Tension tightened my limbs and crackled through the air like lightening.

"Snake, please."

Snake's hand slipped beneath my jacket, his warm palm squeezing my breast. His thumb was rubbing lazily over my nipple, the touch slow and not insistent.

He didn't make any other moves, but kept teasing my nipple until my breathing hitched, warmth spreading through my limbs and the tell-tale ache of desire building in my stomach.

I inhaled, arching my body up into his hand.

He adjusted his body over mine, mouth coming down to claim mine in a hard, quick kiss.

"It's Isaac."

I blinked. "What?"

"My name. Isaac. I want to hear it from your pretty mouth when you come."

I moaned, biting my bottom lip as his body moved lower over mine. His hands snagged the waistband of my leggings, tugging insistently.

I lifted my hips off the bed so he could peel them off my legs. The cool air that rushed over my heated skin made me gasp.

He pulled everything off—leggings, socks, booties—I heard them clatter to the floor. And then he was kneeling on the floor between my slightly parted legs.

I still had my underwear on. It wasn't exactly "fuck me" underwear, more what you would call utilitarian underwear, cotton, comfortable, full briefed, and baby blue.

Snake did not appear dissuaded by my unimpressive undergarments, though, if the look in his eyes was anything to go on.

The slight stubble on his cheek scraped across my inner thigh as he turned to press a hot kiss to the inside of my knee.

My legs were shaking.

This was new, exciting territory that hadn't been tainted by my ex-boyfriend. Hunter would have *never*.

Snake's warm, soft hands skimmed my calves and up my thighs; his fingers hooked into the waistband of my underwear.

"Is this okay?" he asked, breath skittering across my skin, raising goose bumps on my arms.

"God, yes," I rasped.

He tugged on my underwear and again I lifted my hips so he could pull them off my body and discard them.

Snake crowded closer to me, his shoulders pushing my knees farther apart, spreading me before his gaze.

He ran a finger casually through my slick folds, humming with appreciation. "So wet, sweetheart."

I whimpered as his finger explored me, pressing inside, thumb rolling my clit. "Do you want me to eat this pretty pussy, Sheenah?"

Oh, God. I pressed one of my hands over my eyes. His words were so *dirty*, something straight out of a dirty fanfic. I couldn't help the response they kindled in my body; I writhed under his fingers and his gaze and his words.

I knew he was going to make me say it so I just breathed, "Yes."

I very much wanted that; I very much wanted his filthy, plump mouth on my sex.

Snake kissed a hot line down my stomach, along the inside of my thigh, taking his sweet damn time getting to the point.

His hot breath fanned lightly over my pussy, causing me to let out a low groan. I felt him opening my outer lips, one of his fingers running tantalizingly slowly from clit to entrance. Using my own wetness, his finger rubbed over the tight opening between the cleft of my cheeks and I bucked.

He chuckled darkly, bracing his free arm across my lower abdomen to keep me where he wanted me.

His tongue flicked over my clit and I pulled my scarf over my face so that I could moan into the material.

His tongue continued its light pressure as his fingers invaded me, first one and then two and then three until I squirmed against his hand as he pumped. He worked me until my breath was coming in short, sharp, needy gasps and I was writhing against his hold.

I felt the sensation start to build again, my whole body drawing up tight as a bow string. When his lips closed over my clit and sucked and his finger crooked inside me, I exploded with a loud cry that was muffled by my scarf.

Snake crawled his way back up my body, teeth nipping as he went, lips pressing quickly to mine before he fell onto his back with a puff of air.

He left the taste of me on my lips.

It took me a minute to catch my breath after that. And then I realized it was a little weird that I was only naked from the waist down and Snake wasn't nearly naked enough. Should I get the rest of the way naked? Should I tell him thank you? If anyone deserved to be thanked for his efforts, it was definitely Snake.

To stall for time—and because I wasn't sure what to do next—I made myself a bit more comfortable and discarded the scarf and jacket on the floor. I turned into Snake, curling my body along the side of his.

"You know, I think it's about your turn." I slid my chilled fingers up his warm shirt.

He laughed, eyes still closed. "I'm okay."

I raised a skeptical eyebrow. "Are you sure? Do most guys go so long without...relief?"

He cracked an eyelid open at me. "I didn't say that." He rolled over onto his side so that we were nose to nose on the bed. "I jack myself off every time you leave. Sometimes more than once." His thumb ran over my bottom lip. "I jack off just thinking about you when you're not here. I jack myself off just thinking about all the things I want to do to you."

My face had to be as red as a tomato at this point. "Oh."

His hand skimmed down my side, over my hip, fingers kneading into my still-bare ass. "But I'm willing to wait and go at your pace. Whatever you need."

So many questions hovered on my tongue. I wanted to ask him why. Why was he willing to wait for me? Why was he so accommodating? Why didn't he push?

Snake rubbed his thumb at the spot between my eyebrows. "What are you thinking about so hard?"

I swatted his hand away. "Stop figuring out my tells."

"It was pretty obvious." He smiled.

"Why?" I blurted. "Why are you willing to go at my pace?"

His brows arched. "Because I'm not a dick?"

"But you barely know me."

"Am I supposed to be a dick because I barely know you? I'm getting to know you."

"But...why?"

He gathered my hands up in his and held them together between us, almost like we were in prayer. "You're someone I want to know."

I opened my mouth again, ready to let some more whys come out, but he put a finger to my lips to stop me.

"You're worth knowing, Sheenah Green-Barnes, baggage or no baggage. You're worth knowing."

Something cracked in my chest that may have been the walls I'd so carefully put up around my heart. I felt simultaneously heavy and light. I felt like crying. I felt like kissing Snake until our lips were bruised.

He saw something in me that I was still unable to see in myself. Something that I thought was lost to me.

I wanted to be the girl he thought he saw. The girl worth knowing. I didn't know if I could find her.

CHAPTER TWELVE

OKAY I'M OKAY

Rayme and I showed up early to the studio to set up the backdrops and lighting. I brought snacks and cold brew for all my people.

Rayme grabbed one of the cold brews as soon as they finished setting up their lights and tipped it towards me. "Bless."

I set up a small changing area and carefully arranged the dress rack that contained the Medusa next to on a short table.

I heard Vivien before I saw her.

Her deep, distinctive laugh sounded just right outside the door before she entered, followed by the biggest man I'd ever seen.

I'd of course seen pictures of Tobias on Vivien's social media, but that really didn't compare to seeing him in the flesh.

He towered almost a head and a half over Vivien, and even I had to look up to meet his eyes.

Rayme muttered "Oh, shit" from somewhere around my elbow and their wide-eyed gaze told me they were also impressed.

Tobias was really pretty, with his flowing hair, dazzling smile, and sparkling blue eyes—no wonder he had Vivien in a tizzy.

"SheeBee!" she squealed, wrapping me up in a tight hug.

I was still staring at Tobias, who was hovering behind her with his indulgent smile. "Sorry, I'm distracted."

Vivien flushed prettily, and she gestured to Tobias. "This is Sheenah, my bestie."

"I've heard so much about you," he rumbled, holding out his gigantic paw for me to shake.

I did and then I was bumped unceremoniously out of the way by one of Rayme's slender hips.

"Rayme, the photographer," they purred, batting their eyelashes and holding their camera up for proof.

I almost let out a snort-laugh, but Tobias was not fazed at all.

"Lovely to meet you too," he said.

"Well, we need to get started," I said, grabbing Rayme by the shoulders and bodily directing them back towards our setup.

"How are they both so fucking hot?" they mused.

This time I did snort; they were not wrong.

I had watched Vivien go from a slumped wallflower, always curled into herself, to a bold and loud live wire, who wasn't afraid to take up space.

It was refreshing to see her glow under Tobias's devoted gaze as he tutted and fretted about her, holding her bag and phone and sunglasses.

Watching them together made my chest feel weird. It was hard to identify the feeling. I don't think it was quite jealousy—Vivien deserved to be happy. I don't think I was jealous of her happiness—or maybe I was.

Maybe I was jealous of the way Tobias looked at her. Like she was the entirety of his world. Like he didn't need anything else. Like she was air.

"Where do I strip?" Vivien's question brought me back to the task at hand.

I pointed her towards the curtain I'd set up and followed her with the Medusa.

As soon as we were covered, she started peeling off her chunky sweater and leggings. "Are you sure I can't wear any makeup?"

I shook my head. "Nope. I'm going to get your hair wet, too."

She frowned at me, leggings dangling from her hand. "Excuse me?"

"Indeed." I started unwrapping my couture gown. I had been inspired by Giavonna's swamp witches for Vivien's styling for the shoot.

I wanted her bare, stripped down, barefoot, in contrast with the high-fashion gown.

"It's a good thing I love you," she grumbled.

"You're gonna look stunning. Just trust me. Now, get into this thing."

I helped Vivien into the gown, strapping her in with the laces and zipper. I had made a few adjustments to the design since our last fitting, but the corset still fit like a glove. I added more height and structure to the bust, so that it almost looked like a piece of armor.

The base of the gown was still black, but I had created a nude overlay with embroidered roses. The slit ran clean up to the crease of her thigh and I had made the train significantly more dramatic.

Vivien swished the fabric with her hands. "Sheenah, you've really outdone yourself. It's gorgeous."

I huffed out a sigh of relief that we had finally made it to this point. "It sure better be. My application is riding on this bad boy."

"They'd be out of their minds not to accept you."

I wished I had her confidence.

Vivien emerged from behind the curtain to gasps from Rayme and Tobias, and I had to stifle a grin. They both wore identical thunderstruck expressions.

I held out a hand. "I'm not even done yet!"

"It gets *better*?" Rayme asked.

I motioned for Vivien to take down her bun.

She sighed but did it anyway, tossing the hair tie to Tobias.

I wrapped a towel around her shoulders and then grabbed my spray bottle, aiming it threateningly at her face. "You ready?"

She eyed the bottle with distaste. "The things I do for you."

"Close your eyes!" I chirped.

She did, and I started in with the spray bottle.

It was a tedious task; I wanted her hair wet, but I didn't want to soak it all at once because I didn't want water on the Medusa. And Vivien had a lot of hair.

I had to do it meticulously and in chunks. I let it run down her face—which made her grumble—and it made tracks in the makeup she had sneaked on, thinking I wouldn't notice her cat eyes, I guessed?

"Hold still," I said. Then I rubbed my thumbs across her eyelids.

"My lashes!" she squealed. I heard Tobias laugh.

"You can keep them, but I'm smudging your liner."

I sprayed more water on her face, smudging the black eyeliner and mascara with my thumbs as I went.

Once I was finished, I soaked up any loose water that clung to the ends of her hair with the towel. Then I gathered all the soaked strands and laid them gently down her back, so there was nothing to distract from the bodice of the gown.

I heard a click and then a flash.

"Yeah, that's hot," Rayme said. "Let's get this party started."

Taking the wet towel with me, I backed away to the sidelines to let Rayme and Vivien work. My presence would only be required if something on the gown needed to be adjusted.

Vivien looked devastating. And also like her head had just been dunked in a bucket of water and slightly pissed, but still devastating. It was perfect.

I gave her a thumbs-up.

She gave me the finger, but her lips curled in a ghost of a smile.

I sidled up to Tobias as Rayme and Vivien got to work.

He was watching with his arms crossed, muscles bulging, barely contained by the buffalo check flannel shirt he wore.

He looked like a lumber snack.

I was only able to watch from the sidelines for a few minutes before Rayme gestured for me to come in and adjust the Medusa and help Vivien change her pose for some different angles. I fiddled with her hair, so some of it fell over her shoulders.

"Come take a look at these," Rayme said, angling the camera towards me so I could take a look at what they had so far.

"Perfect," I said. "Make sure you show off the train, Vivi."

"Got it, boss," Vivien chirped, gathering up the trailing fabric in her hands for some more dramatic posing.

They started again and I retreated to the sidelines.

Tobias had gone missing while we were fiddling with Vivien.

In the middle of Rayme hollering at Vivien to make love to the camera—which was causing her to break into giggles—Tobias reappeared with a carrying tray of four cold drinks. By the look of the dollops of whipped cream on the top, they were strawberry frappuccinos.

Both Rayme and Vivien squealed when they spotted the drinks.

"Hold up, you!" I pointed to Vivien, who was attempting to make a quick break for the drinks.

I grabbed a clean towel from the pile I had bought and wrapped it around her neck like a bib. Both Rayme and Tobias snorted.

"Don't drip on the couture," I huffed.

Vivien's hand fled up to her heart dramatically. "I would *never* drip on the couture."

Then she leaned over and sipped delicately from the straw as Tobias held her drink away from her body.

"I appreciate that," I said dryly as I sipped on my own drink. There was just something so refreshing about free drinks, never mind that we were on our second overpriced cold drink of the day.

C'est la vie, as they said.

After a quick break, I hustled everyone back to the photo shoot and the task at hand.

"Babe..." Vivien looked at Tobias. "Can you get some behind-the-scenes shots?"

He nodded without protest and grabbed Vivien's phone—and I knew it was hers by the ostentatious glittery case—out of her bag. She swiped to unlock and Tobias took up a spot on the periphery of the shoot, phone in hand like a professional. Definitely like he'd done this before.

I peeked over his shoulder. "She likes downward angles."

He grinned. "Oh, I know."

I patted his broad shoulder. "Of course you do."

About an hour later, we wrapped up the shoot, and I felt like I had plenty of choices to showcase the Medusa for my application portfolio. After all, Rayme and Vivien were both very good at what they did. Vivien and the dress were both showstoppers.

Vivien was laughing and her cheeks were tinged pink. She wiggled a little in joy as we went back behind my makeshift changing station, me holding the massive train of the dress so it didn't drag on the floor.

"That was so much fun!"

She stopped and propped her hands on her hips, waiting for me to unlace the dress and let her out.

I felt something like relief. One more task accomplished. One more thing I could take off my to-do list and mental load.

I started pulling on the laces, but Vivien shot me a devious look over her shoulder. "So."

I felt my cheeks redden even though she hadn't said anything else or asked any questions. "So."

"You haven't given me any updates about your boy."

I finished unlacing her, holding up the sides of the bodice so that she could step out. "He's not my boy."

Her dark, perfectly sculpted eyebrows rose and her mouth quirked. Something in the tone of my voice must have put that look on her face. "Mm-hmm."

I sighed, wrapping the Medusa up safe and sound again while Vivien pulled back on all her clothes.

"Do you have time for lunch?"

She pulled her damp hair back up into a messy bun. "I'm already ahead of you. Apparently, there's a used bookstore around here somewhere that Tobias wants to check out. So, I have a few hours while he wanders."

After we said goodbye to Rayme and Tobias, we dropped my supplies back off at my apartment and then holed up at the little diner where my friend Jenna worked, although she was off today.

Vivien's mouth hung open, a fry paused in midair in shock. "Are you telling me"—the fry dropped to her plate—"that you got a tattoo to get a boy's attention?"

My face was burning. I had a lot to catch her up on. I swirled one of my fries in the smear of mayo across my plate. "Well, it sounds bad when you put it that way."

"Don't get me wrong, I love tattoos. But it was kind of...impulsive? I don't know. I guess there are worse reasons to get inked."

"It's really good, though."

Sabbath Ink had a picture of my line work on their Instagram page, so I pulled it up for her to see.

She nodded in approval. "Oh yeah, that's gorgeous, Shee." She peered a little closer at the picture. "He's really, really good."

"I know." I felt a little puff of pride, even though I wasn't sure why I was feeling pride. It wasn't like it was my work. Maybe I was just glad she didn't think it was atrocious and that I had completely lost my damn mind.

She grinned at me conspiratorially. "Do you have any pictures of the man himself?"

Snake showed up every once in a while on Sabbath's Ink's feed, but he didn't seem to keep much of a social media presence himself. I knew because I had looked.

I held up a finger. "Hold on."

"Oh, I am holding with barely contained excitement."

I scrolled back through Sabbath Ink's feed until I found the pictures from the gallery opening on Halloween. I was in a couple candid shots, but Niyah had taken individual photos of all the artists in front of their work.

I found Snake's and flipped the phone back around.

Vivien bit off half a fry. "My, my. Ain't he a compact hottie."

I laughed, the tight bubble of anxiety in my chest loosening. I didn't know why I was so nervous to tell her about Snake, but I felt pleased with her approval.

"I don't think they like being called compact."

She shrugged. "I could just call him short."

"Not all of us can find man mammoths. You really should save the tall ones for us freakishly tall girls."

"I've already called dibs. *Thoroughly.*"

I snorted into my Coke and had to wipe my nose on my sleeve. "How did Thanksgiving go, by the way?"

"About as well as it could go. Mom really liked Tobias, so that was a plus." She rolled her eyes. "Although, I'm pretty sure she was about to ask him what he saw in me but managed to contain herself at the last second. She grilled him on how we met."

"That's weird."

"Yeah, well, I think she was baffled that he just saw me and wanted to talk to me."

"I thought y'all were doing better."

She snorted. "Yeah, well, that was better. She didn't make any comments about me eating sweet potato casserole."

"Progress, not perfection," I said, holding up my fork as if to emphasize my point.

Vivien and I had been friends since elementary school, so I had done plenty of growing up and hanging out at her house over the years. Ms. Martin had no qualms about buying snacks and sodas and sweets and watching me consume them. But any time Vivien would reach for something that was bought—but not approved—she'd get The Look.

The Look would cause Vivien to blush and sheepishly put back whatever it was that she had grabbed.

I couldn't ever understand why she wanted to come to my house—at the Cedar Creek Mobile Home Park—and she couldn't understand why I always wanted to be at her house instead.

She clapped her hands at me. "That's enough about my strained relationship with my mother." Her eyes gleamed. "I need to know more about the enigmatic Snake."

I stared down hard at my half-eaten plate of avocado cheeseburger and French fries. Vivien still didn't know all the backstory

I had spilled to Snake. If I could tell a man I barely knew, why then was it still so hard to tell my best friend?

"I have something I need to tell you, and I just need you to listen, okay?"

Vivien nodded, her face solemn.

So, I told her.

I told her about the first time, about all the other times of coercive sex. I told her about the pregnancy and about Hunter telling our parents, even though I had begged him not to. I told her about how happy they were, how Hunter's parents jumped right into finding us our own double wide. I told her about declining my scholarship to Penn Warren and lying to her about why I wouldn't be going away to college as her roommate. I told her about the abortion, and how Hunter reacted when I told him. I told her about how my mom reacted when I told her. How she had broken down into tears because I had "killed her grandbaby" when she hadn't even cried when I told her I'd been assaulted.

Once the words started, they wouldn't stop. There'd be no way I could stop now, or take them back. There was relief in that knowledge.

Vivien's face grew ever more appropriately horrified, which made me feel slightly better about the whole thing.

I finished with "And that's that" before grabbing my straw and taking a long drink of my Coke.

Vivien blinked a few times. "Sheenah, I-I. I knew there was more to the story, but I didn't expect...Jesus. I'd ask if you were okay, but that feels dismissive."

I shrugged. "I am, kinda. I mean, as well as I can be right now." I let out a breath of air, shoulders slumping. "It feels better now that you know."

"Why didn't you tell me? I mean, I know I had a lot going on of my own that year, but I would have supported you. I would have taken you to the clinic. You know I would have."

I nodded, because I knew she would have, I had no doubts about that, now or then.

"It was just..." I cleared my throat, which was suddenly tight. "It was just, I had already told my mom, the person who was supposed to love me most in the world, and she didn't believe me. I couldn't risk you, too."

I pressed the heels of my hands into my eyes.

Vivien grabbed one of my hands, squeezing it hard. "Oh, honey. You know I love you, right?"

I nodded vigorously, not trusting myself to speak. I rubbed a little harder at my eyes and took a deep breath. "Okay. I'm okay. And I love you, too." I gave her a weak smile, to show that I was really okay.

Her expression was skeptical, eyes a little wet around the edges. "Okay, so all that obviously complicates your relationship with Snake."

"Indeed, it does." I appreciated her quick change of subject before we both broke down at the diner table. "I won't give up anything again, Viv. Not for anyone."

She cocked an eyebrow. "It's that serious?"

"No, but..."

"But you like him?"

I sighed. "Yeah, I think I like him."

"And he knows about…" She waved a hand around in the air as if gesturing to all the secrets I'd just revealed.

I felt my face flush. "Uh, yeah. He's been pretty great about it, actually."

"You sound surprised."

I shrugged. "Well, you know, not all guys are willing to go this long without having sex."

"Good. Wait, what." She lowered her voice. "Y'all haven't had sex yet?"

I glanced around to make sure no one was near before leaning forward so I could whisper and still have her hear me. "I mean, we've done…stuff. A lot of stuff. But not like *the*…act."

She grinned. "There are lots of ways to have sex, Sheenah."

"Yes, I'm finding this out."

"Just enjoy the ride, Shee, literally and figuratively." She wiggled her eyebrows at me and I tossed a fry at her.

"You're incorrigible!"

"I know. Listen, I want you to do what's best for you. If you like this guy, like him, and enjoy the process. And all the interesting sex you get to have."

"It just feels disingenuous, I guess. To…date, knowing there's an expiration date."

She shrugged. "That's what dating is."

I threw a couple of fries across my plate. "Says the woman in a committed relationship."

She flushed prettily. "Yeah, but look at how long it took me to get here. And how many guys I had to go through."

I grinned. "Yeah, how many was it? Did you lose count again?"

"Oh, shut up. Oh, shit." She dropped a dollop of ketchup on her expansive bosom. "Look, there's uncertainty in every relationship, I guess, until you get married. And even then, it's still not guaranteed. Do you know how high the divorce rate is now? There are no guarantees." She dabbed at the ketchup with a fry.

"You should put that on an inspirational poster," I grumbled.

"As long as you're both being honest, there's nothing wrong with an expiration date. There's nothing wrong with casual dating. There's nothing wrong with following your vagina."

"Nope. You should put *that* on an inspirational poster."

"I can't claim credit for it."

Her phone suddenly buzzed and she glanced over at it. "Oh, shit, I forgot about Tobias."

"Is he wondering if you're ever coming back?" I laughed.

"He is, but also told me not to rush, so."

"Ugh, how is he so perfect?"

She shrugged. "Beats me."

"And what does he see in you again?"

She chucked a fry at my forehead, where it bounced off harmlessly. "Did you or did you not read my how-to on blow jobs?"

I shuffled my feet across the linoleum floor. "I did," I confessed quietly.

"Well, now you know." She gave me an exaggerated wink before pulling out her wallet. "Let's go rescue him."

CHAPTER THIRTEEN

A FOOL'S ERRAND

After my visit with Vivien, I felt really good about my application portfolio to GSAD but even more confused about my feelings about Snake.

Rayme had an extremely quick turnaround when it came to going through their footage and they had a zipped folder of edited photos emailed to me the next day.

Vivien and the Medusa were stunning. Ethereal. Dangerous. It was going to be hard to pick the best ones for the application.

Snake was another matter entirely.

I didn't know what we were doing, and that made me feel off-balanced, uncertain. I think the uncertainty was what worried me the most. We were fooling around, yes, but after the last time I saw him, it also felt like more than that.

Maybe I should just tell him about GSAD and get it over with. But that would presume that I got accepted and Snake saw something in this relationship besides casually hooking up.

What if he didn't even care that I was planning to move away? That'd sting, wouldn't it?

The least I could do was put my cards on the table and let him decide for himself. That would be the mature, responsible thing to do.

I chewed on my thumbnail and checked my phone; I needed to get to the library before they closed and find some resources for my term paper. Maybe I could see Snake after.

I opened his chat thread.

> Are you working tonight?

His answer came almost immediately.

> Unfortunately, yes.

> Ugh, that sucks.

> You don't have to
> tell me that.
> I want to see you.
> I'm hard just thinking
> about coming on your perky tits.

Oh, no.

I chewed harder on the side of my fingernail, squeezing my thighs together. I had never sexted before in my life. What was something sexy to say back? What if he thought it wasn't sexy? Why was this so complicated?

I shall very much enjoy that, I responded after one excruciating long minute. *Shall? What the fuck was that, Sheenah? Was I in a period drama now?*

I rubbed a nervous palm back and forth on my thigh, waiting for Snake's response.

In came a string of crying-laughing faces.

That was awful.

> *Omg I'm so sorry.*

Was it possible to die from embarrassment, because I'm pretty sure I was now dead from embarrassment.

> *Can we try that again?*

Sure. I mean, it can't get worse than that, can it?

I snorted out loud, thumbs hovering over the keyboard, trying my best to think of something to say. My skin burned with the thoughts of all I could ask him to do to me.

Agency, Sheenah. You can ask for what you want. You can get what you want.

My phone had gone dark waiting for me to make up my mind. Snake hadn't texted again, and I imagined him just patiently waiting on my response, as he'd done all along.

I opened the chat again and typed out one sentence, quickly, before I could lose my nerve.

> *I want you to fuck me.*

> *See you at 10.*

The local library wasn't that big and their section on poets—women poets in particular—was not that extensive.

It didn't take me long to check out a few books that should give me a decent start on my resources for Howard's term paper. We were required to have a minimum of five physical sources that didn't come from an article on the internet.

I stowed my books away in my bag and headed back to my apartment, trying not to dwell on the fact that I still had five hours before I was able to see Snake.

It was probably a bad idea to get so revved up so early. Because now I had nothing to do but wait.

I paced a quick, anxious circle around my small apartment before an idea occurred to me.

I brought out my phone and texted Rayme.

> *What are you doing?*
> *I need help. ASAP.*

> *What's up, hon?*

> *I need to go*

shopping...

For what?

Uh...lingerie?

*Is that a question
lololol*

*Lingerie. Yes.
Like, hot stuff*

*Is it for
your man crush?*

Yes

*MISSION ACCEPTED
Be there in 5*

I met Rayme downstairs and hopped in their small sedan.

Rayme tossed their phone on my lap, which was already pulled up to the maps app, the little blue line snaking across the screen.

"I did a little recon. There's nowhere to buy decent stuff in this podunk town, but I found a little boutique we can try."

I nodded, nervous again, rubbing my palms on my jeans. I didn't do lingerie or sexy undergarments. I wore the underwear that came in a cotton five-pack. I dressed for myself. The idea of dressing for someone, dressing to titillate, was a different ballgame.

"So..." Rayme merged onto the expressway. "What are you looking for?"

"Uh, I'm not sure. I guess, like an outfit?"

They nodded. "Okay, so we want all the stops. Theme?"

"I have to pick a theme?"

Rayme laughed, nose ring catching the afternoon light. "Okay, I see I'm working with a total noob. Well, are you going for frilly, floral, goth, classy? Slutty?"

I put my face in my hands and groaned. "This was a bad idea."

"This was a great idea. I've got you."

We arrived at the boutique—Carmilla's—and were greeted by a short older woman, with white hair like a dandelion fluff.

Rayme smiled and quickly told her we didn't need any help, and then they started pulling things off racks, willy-nilly.

"No white!" I squeaked, when I saw them pick a bridal-white teddy.

Rayme put it back, eyeing me up and down. "We want something to really emphasize that body."

I blushed.

Emphasizing my body was not something I usually spent much time doing. I was a practitioner of body neutrality, especially after so many years of being told my body was evil and needed to be covered up. My body was just a body; it got me to where I was going. But that was before Snake made me feel things I didn't know I was capable of feeling.

I squared my shoulders and joined Rayme in the hunt for something that I would feel good in.

Once our arms were full, the lady working let us into a dressing room.

I shot down some of Rayme's picks before they even hung them up in the room. There was one baby pink one with a frilly skirt that screamed nymphette and that was a hard no.

True to their word, Rayme had selected a wide variety of choices in different styles, colors, and moods.

I sifted through the lace, looking for something that spoke to me.

"You actually have to try one on and come out here," Rayme hollered from where they waited outside the dressing room.

I was uncomfortable and couldn't pinpoint exactly why. I loved clothes. I loved designing them, and drawing them; I loved making beautiful things and these were all beautiful.

I didn't think it was the lingerie.

I think it was the overt sexuality of the lingerie and what that meant.

I was uncomfortable basking in my own overt sexuality. I wasn't covering up my body to protect my modesty. I was unveiling it.

Hunter had treated me like a body to be used; my mom had treated me like a vessel to be used.

These weren't things I wanted.

Snake treated me like a person; my comfort, safety, desire, were paramount, important.

Hangers clacked together as I moved and discarded set after set, until, finally, the last one caught my attention.

It was blood red lace and there were at least three pieces.

"I don't know if I know how to put this thing on," I hollered.

I heard Rayme snort. "Try and we'll fix it."

I shucked everything but my full brief underwear and did my best to pull the other pieces on my body.

The top was a halter style, which I already knew flattered my smaller chest. The panties felt infinitesimally tiny, barely coming up to my belly button. The garter belt was almost as big as the panties and fit snugly around my middle, straps dangling down my thighs, ready for the matching stockings.

"Are you ready?" I called, taking a deep breath.

"Never been readier!"

I peeked around the curtain, on the lookout for any other customers, and then pulled it back, stepping out.

Rayme's eyes widened and then they grinned. "The socks and granny panties are a nice touch."

I felt my chest flush. "Shut up. Well?"

I held my arms out and gave a little twirl.

"Stunning, really."

I pulled at the garter belt. "Are you sure?"

"Girl, I am sure. I wouldn't steer you wrong. You look good enough to eat." They smirked.

Warmth curled in my belly at the thought.

My lingerie set with the matching stockings—because of course I had to get the matching stockings to go with the garter belt—only set me back by about one hundred and fifty dollars, which was a small price to pay for the way I felt in the set.

When I got home it was eight thirty, which meant I still had over an hour before Snake was due to show up.

Which was still way too much time for me to get lost in my thoughts.

I stripped off my alleged granny panties, cut the tags off my fancy set, and pulled everything on. The lace was a little itchy against my skin, but I guess that's what I got for only spending a hundred and fifty on the whole thing.

Stockings pinned and garter on, I twirled again before the weathered standing mirror by my dresser. I had exactly one pair of patent leather heels that might match the vibe of the set, but I kind of liked the stockings and bare feet.

I put my hands on my hips and down again. Turned my hips and then turned them back. Trying out a myriad of different poses in order to land on one that would sufficiently impress Snake when he showed up at my door and I answered in *this*.

It was a fool's errand.

I did not feel sexy. I did not feel alluring. I did not feel desirable. I felt gangly. I felt like I was trying too hard.

I felt like I needed a drink to make this happen.

There was an unopened bottle of Roscato on top of the fridge; I twisted the top off, and poured almost half the bottle into a reusable plastic cup I got from the coffee shop.

The bottles of Roscato weren't that big; half a bottle was barely nothing.

I could hold a little bit of sweet wine.

I could not hold my wine.

A whole bottle of wine later and I was feeling much, much better. I had found a playlist of moody music on YouTube, which I played on the TV, and had rustled up exactly five partially burnt candles and lined them up on the counter. They each had a different smell—which was smelly—but the dancing flames made me giggle.

Tipsy and wine-flushed, with the lights down low, I greatly enjoyed the reflection in the mirror.

Snake's familiar rap on the door shook me out of my self-contemplation and I practically skipped to open the door.

"Snakey!" I yelled, completely forgetting about my plan to greet him all sexy-like.

His eyes widened as he took me in in all my glory, practically hanging off the door. He was zipped up in his black leather jacket and wrapped in tight black jeans. His signature spicy smell tickled my nostrils as I drank in the delicious sight of him.

I jumped into his arms and he caught me with a muffled *oof*, his warm hands curving over the backs of my thighs.

He kicked the door closed.

I buried my nose in his neck. "You smell delicious."

He chuckled. "Aren't you a sight."

"Do you like it?" I asked against his throat.

He hummed, his chest rumbling against mine with the vibration. My body was already warm and languid, but I felt a very acute pressure start forming in my core, nipples furling into tight buds.

He walked me to the bed, dropping me onto it while I giggled. I spread my arms and legs like a starfish.

"I'm ready to be fucked," I said, with a triumphant smile.

His lips curved. He unzipped his jacket, letting it fall off his sculpted arms to puddle on the floor. He leaned down, his knee bracing on the bed between my legs. His warm breath fluttered over the shell of my ear.

My body hummed.

"Are you drunk?"

His nose traced along my jaw and I giggled some more.

"What, no."

"Hmm." His warm lips traced mine and I licked him.

"Okay, maybe just a smidgey. Like, just a smidgey."

I held up my hand, index finger and thumb a hairsbreadth apart to illustrate my point.

His lips touched mine, sweet and tender. My body and my brain were all warm and fuzzy and I arched into his body like a cat, twining my arms around his neck.

His tongue slipped into my mouth and I gave it a little nip. He chuckled again, rubbing his body against mine.

"I'm not going to fuck you while you're drunk." He said it softly, with a hint of amusement coloring his words.

I had wrapped both of my legs around one of his and was rubbing myself against his hard thigh. I immediately stopped, even though my body was screaming at me to do something about the throbbing ache between my legs.

"Why not?" I demanded.

He booped his nose against mine, liquid brown eyes burning. "The whole 'because I'm not a dick' thing again, I'm afraid."

"But I'm ready," I whined, wriggling my body in what I hope was a suggestive way and not reminiscent of a floundered fish.

He just laughed again, kissed me chastely on the cheek, and said, "Stay ready, then."

I starfished again with a whine as he removed his warm body from off the top of mine.

"Coffee or water?" he asked, moving towards the kitchen.

"I work in a coffee shop. I don't keep coffee in my home," I groused.

"Water it is, then," he said with an amused lilt to his voice.

I heard him rustling around for a glass and then the kitchen sink turned on. The annoying ache was still between my legs and I rubbed my thighs together to try to relieve some of the pressure. And also in frustration.

Snake arrived by the side of my bed holding a glass of water. "Drink."

He was so bossy. I sat up anyway and chugged half the glass, giving him the dirtiest look I could muster.

His beautiful eyes just laughed and danced at me, thick lips curving slightly up at one side in a smirk. "Don't look at me like that." He put the half-empty glass of water on the end table. "It's not that I don't want to fuck you, it's that I won't right now."

He just threw around the word *fuck* so casually, in his raspy, bossy voice, it made my toes tingle.

I frowned. "That sounds the same."

"It's not."

He started unbuttoning his jeans and I jumped up to my knees, but he held a finger up. "Don't get excited."

I threw my hands up in frustration. "Too late!"

"I'm just getting comfortable. Lie down."

I immediately did as I was told, curling up into a half-moon, and his warm body curled up behind me. He tucked me into his body, throwing one of his heavy legs over mine.

I wriggled.

He swatted gently at my butt. "Stop."

I huffed out a breath and pouted.

He tugged the crocheted throw blanket that I kept on the end of my bed over us both, one of his hands brushing my hair back from my face.

I couldn't deny that this was nice.

His hand stroked down my hair, down my arm, down the length of my body in a gentle rhythm. It was damn pleasant. Soothing.

I sighed, snuggling into the arm he'd tucked up under my head. His warmth and smell engulfed me, wrapping around and through my body until I was certain I'd drown in him.

His hand stopped moving and I made a sound of protest, but he tucked it against my sternum, against the beating of my heart.

"So," he started, voice whisper-quiet as if to not disturb the gentle peace he'd wrought with his petting. "What's all this for?"

The fingers at my sternum plucked at the lace of the halter top.

I let out a small sigh. "You."

His chuckled breath fluttered across the back of my neck. "Why?"

I tried to shrug, which was a struggle to do in our current position, with him wrapped around me. I wasn't sure if I could walk him through my thought process without sounding like a total loon.

"I already like the way you look," he added.

I shook my head, cheek brushing against his arm. "It's not about the way I look."

"What's it about, then?"

I kind of hated this about him—he was way too intuitive for his own good, and probably my own good too. He didn't let things slide; he didn't let me hide behind flimsy excuses. Behind my own fears and hang-ups.

I shifted again in his arms, the motion uncomfortable this time instead of provocative.

"I'm...nervous." The buzz from the wine was unfortunately wearing off—it wasn't very strong wine—but it still felt easier to talk to him this way, not facing each other, my gaze focused on a random, unimportant spot on the ceiling. "I want to...you know...but I'm nervous."

"Why?"

Always that question, why.

I let out a puff of air. "I've only been with one guy and it's not like it was good."

That seemed to stall him. I could feel him thinking, could feel the tension in his limbs.

I was also scared, scared of the way he made my body feel, but I wasn't drunk enough to let that little nugget escape.

"Are you worried it's not going to be good?"

Was that a hint of wounded pride I detected in his voice? It made me laugh. "No, I'm sure *you're* good. What if I'm not?"

"Experience isn't everything. Some people have lots and lots of sex and never get any good at it."

"That tracks."

"Listen to me." Snake tugged on my shoulders until I had rolled all the way around and we were face to face again. The dim lighting in my apartment cast half his face in shadows; the other half was deadly serious. "You're in charge. We're only going to do what you're comfortable with. And I'm going to make you come so many times you're going to be begging me to stop. Do you understand me?"

I felt my whole body flush and I had to avert my eyes because I couldn't hold his intense stare.

I was still so uncomfortable owning my own sexuality, my own wants and needs and desires. I wasn't supposed to. That's not what good girls did.

Snake grabbed my chin and tilted my face up to look at him again. "Understand?"

"Yes."

He pecked my forehead. "Good. Now sleep it off."

Chapter Fourteen

I HAVEN'T BEGGED YET

I woke up with something hard and rigid poking me in the stomach. It didn't take a rocket scientist to figure out what *that* was.

But I had to pee something fierce.

It was surprisingly easy to fall asleep in Snake's arms, the gentle rise and fall of his chest soothing in a way that I wasn't going to spend much time pondering.

I slid out of the bed and tiptoed to the bathroom for a quick refresh. We couldn't have been asleep for more than a couple hours, but my hair looked like I'd been passed out for twelve hours. I brushed it out and braided it quickly, tidying up my eye makeup in the process.

Then I stripped off my stockings and garter belt because they were digging into the sensitive meat of my thighs. And they were itchy.

I slunk back to bed, trying not to jostle Snake too much as I climbed back in and under the throw blanket.

He had turned over on his back during my brief absence, one arm splayed across his abdomen. He was wearing only a soft Sabbath Ink tee and navy blue, tight, boxer briefs. I resisted the urge to take a peek under the blanket at what had been poking me.

He was extremely handsome in sleep, face soft and unlined.

I traced the arch of his eyebrows, down the bridge of his nose, over his lips. I traced the ridges of his biceps, the curved and inked lines of his forearms, the hard seams of his knuckles. I traced the hard muscles of his chest, fingertip running over one of his nipples. I did it again and then stopped.

"Don't stop now," he said and I squeaked, snatching my hand away.

"How long have you been awake?"

"Since you got up." He grinned, cracking one eye open. "Do continue."

"You could have said something," I accused.

He shrugged and rearranged himself, so that he was flat on his back on the bed, arms crossed behind his head. "I didn't want you to stop touching me."

I harrumphed, but Snake was looking at me. Just lying there in repose, waiting.

"Fine," I said, but he still didn't react. A small smile tugged at his lips.

Fine, I told myself, *you can do this*.

I splayed my hand on his hard abdomen, fingertips tugging up the hem of his shirt. They brushed across warm skin and the soft hair covering his lower belly.

And then I went lower and I may have stopped breathing.

The length beneath my hand was hard and hot and pulsing with its own life. It jumped and grew as I stroked and I heard Snake's breath go ragged.

I was possessed with an overwhelming urge to finally see it, after all this time. I pushed away the throw blanket and pulled at Snake's boxers; he lifted his hips in silence to accommodate me. I tossed the boxers away into the ether where the rest of our clothes went.

Snake's cock wasn't particularly long; it was short and thick, kind of like him. I gripped him around the base, and he gave a small, almost involuntary thrust.

I stroked down to the dusky head and ran my thumb over the slit, where a bead of slick moisture had formed.

Snake wasn't lying quietly in silent repose anymore. His arms were bunched at his side, hands fisted in the comforter, eyes glued to where my fingers played. I thumbed through the slit again, watching the reaction of his face.

"What do you like?" I asked, stroking down again now that my fingers were wet.

His chest was heaving. "Whatever you want to do. I like whatever you want to do."

"That's not very specific," I teased, as I continued to stroke him, tightening my grip.

"I...can't think," he ground out, voice raspy and thick.

I felt powerful, in control, like right after I socked Colton in the nose. Having Snake writhing under my touch was going straight to my head. His cock throbbed in time to the throbbing in my pussy.

An image flashed through my head—him ejaculating all over my chest, across the pretty lace pattern of my top.

I adjusted my grip, testing out different types of pressure and holds, while Snake panted above me, hips barely restrained from bucking into my hand.

"Jesus fucking Christ, Sheenah," he growled, head tipping back, tendons stark in his neck.

I grinned, continuing my exploration. The head was positively leaking now, so I ran my fingers through it, pressing gently on the slit.

I got the fingers on my other hand wet, using them to rub gently over his hot and smooth balls, while I stroked a steady rhythm with the other hand.

My fingers traveled further, down that liminal space between his sac and the tight, puckered hole between his sculpted cheeks.

He let out a sound that I'd never heard come out of a person before. Something torn and gargled, animalistic and keening.

I slipped my finger in, lubricated by his own arousal, crooking it at the second knuckle while I squeezed down his shaft.

This time his hips did buck and with a ragged groan he exploded under my fingers, hot semen coating my hand and splashing against my chest.

Snake's body had stilled, a sheen of sweat on his forehead and down his exposed arms. He was staring up at the ceiling with a dazed look on his face.

"Was that...good?" I asked tentatively. All evidence would point towards *yes* but it's not like I had much experience with these things.

"Jesus," he growled, suddenly sitting up and pulling his T-shirt off his head. He used it to wipe off my hand (but not my chest), his burning gaze never leaving mine. "Take it off."

"Take what off?" My mouth was dry.

"Everything. Take everything off." His gaze was hot, hungry, searing a hole through every part of me.

His scrutiny felt like a tangible thing, sliding over my face, my neck, my cum-covered breasts, my belly, my heat, still hidden by the wine-red lace.

I nodded, hands going to the delicate ties that barely held the halter top to my body. It fell with a quiet susurration.

Snake moved closer, grabbed the top and discarded it off the side of the bed. We were both on our knees facing each other.

"Panties. Now."

His voice was soft but there was no denying the command there, or the way my hands itched to obey him.

I'd examine that particular urge later.

I slid my hands down the sides of the lacy panties, tugging them off my legs one by one and throwing them in the direction the top went.

I was fully exposed, the cool air and Snake's heated gaze turning my nipples into hard little peaks.

His hands followed where his gaze was going earlier. Tracing along my jaw, down the line of my throat, my collarbones, smearing through the sticky cum that still lingered on my chest. His fingers rolled one of my nipples between them, teasing and tugging on the tight bud until I sighed.

Both hands ran down the backs of my arms, pulling them towards him. He caressed the back of each hand with his thumbs, pulling them to his mouth and kissing each palm. His lips burned my palms like fire.

"Sheenah," he rumbled and it was only then that I realized I had closed my eyes. I was awash with a sensation that felt too big for my body to contain. So many tangled thoughts and feelings, Snake's touch like tiny pinpricks on my skin. Hunter's voice, my mom's voice, my pastor's voice echoing in my head, telling me how shameful I was, how dangerous. Dirty, ruined, impure, soiled, damaged goods.

"Sheenah, sweetheart, are you okay?" The concerned note in Snake's voice finally made my eyes snap open and only then I realized I was looking at him through a glazed window.

I was crying.

Silent tears were running down my face.

I had a hard time finding his eyes through the onslaught of quiet tears. I pulled one of my hands from his, swiping it across my face like I couldn't believe quite what was happening.

It was like a wound I couldn't staunch, but I didn't feel sad.

I felt stripped raw and then pieced back together again.

I swiped at my cheeks again. "I-I'm sorry." And then I laughed. The sound just burst from my chest.

Snake had a mildly concerned look on his face, but I noted that he hadn't let go of my other hand, he hadn't run.

"Do you want to talk about it?" he asked.

I shook my head. "No, I don't want to talk about it."

I slid both of my arms around his neck, crushing our chests together, and then I kissed him.

The kiss was tentative at first, closed lips gliding over closed lips, and I could feel Snake's resistance, the tension in his hard body.

I supposed a naked girl sobbing in front of you could do that to a man.

But I didn't want Snake to be tentative; I didn't want him to be careful and hold me like I was a piece of glass that could shatter into a million pieces at the lightest touch. I didn't want him to feel like he had upset me, because that was the furthest thing that had happened.

I nipped at his lower lip with my teeth and tugged at his hair with my fingers.

A low growl rumbled deep in his throat, vibrating against my own chest since we were pressed so close together.

His hands skimmed across the wings of my shoulder blades and down my sides.

"Spread your legs," he rasped.

My body quivered but I did as he said, spreading my thighs apart and clinging tighter to his neck.

His hand traveled down my spine, across the curve of my ass, and through the tight curls that covered my mound. His fingers parted my flesh, one finger dipping inside to trail through the wetness he found there.

I moaned as he rubbed against my clit, deepening our kiss. He kept up the pressure on my clit, fingers never slowing or gentling, and I writhed on his hand, my arms wrapped tightly around his neck.

His words rasped darkly against my ear. "Are you going to come for me, sweet Sheenah?"

My own arms tightened, my whole body going taut, muscles in my thighs quivering as the orgasm ripped through my body and I finished on a long moan.

Snake continued to hold me tight against him, his cock trapped hot and hard between us, as I rode out the after shock of my orgasm, clenching empty and needy around his fingers.

I had come, but I still wanted more. The fire low in my belly barely felt quenched.

I finally let him go, nudging softly at his chest. "Get a condom."

His brow furrowed, cheeks lightly flushed. "Are you sure?"

"Yes," I said confidently. I wasn't sure about most things in my life, but right now, at this moment, with him coating my skin, I was sure of Snake.

He scrambled off the bed and hunted around on the floor for his pants. After finding what he was looking for, he joined me back on the bed, sitting on the edge.

I watched, mildly fascinated as he opened the condom wrapper and rolled it onto his swollen cock.

Hunter hadn't used condoms. It was probably a small miracle that I only ended up accidentally pregnant once. A part of me wanted to think it was malicious, that he'd done it on purpose. Did he really not know? Or did he really not care? Questions without answers.

There was something extremely mundane but also terribly erotic about the way Snake sheathed himself, wrapping his hand around the base, pinching off the end of the condom.

I moved to lay back on the bed, but a hand on my thigh stopped me.

"No, ride me," he said.

He laid back on the bed, his hand supporting me as I straddled him. I leaned forward, bracing my hands on his hard chest, the head of his cock lined up at my entrance.

Snake put one hand on my hip and took his cock in the other, running it through my wet folds. When it brushed against my swollen clit, we both groaned.

He lined up at my entrance, the head gently nudging inside, and I gasped at the sensation. Now that he was notched, Snake took hold of both my hips, fingertips digging into my skin.

"Slowly," he rasped, a sheen of sweat breaking out on his forehead. "Go slowly."

I bore down, his thick length spearing up inside me in a deliciously slow slide. I moaned, back arching, nails digging into his chest.

"Fuck," I gasped. This is what I had been missing before. I could feel my pussy fluttering against him, against the gentle invasion.

Finally, he was lodged all the way inside and I ground my pelvis against his because it felt like the most natural thing in the world.

A strangled sound left his mouth. "Slow, go slowly. Are you still okay?" His words were ground out from between clenched teeth. He had brought his legs up and I could feel their heat against my back.

I moved my hips again, experimentally, reveling in the tight stretch. His eyelashes fluttered and his hands clenched.

I braced my hands against his knees and let my head fall back. "Never been better," I said through gasps of pleasure.

We stayed in a slow grind for inexorable minutes, just feeling each other, but I could sense Snake's barely restrained control. His hands shook with it.

I needed more. More to push the fluttering pressure in my pussy to full force.

I leaned back down, nipping at the column of his neck with my teeth, nipping at the lobe of his ear. "I'm tired of going slow."

That's when he rolled me, one hand bracing my back.

It was reminiscent of the other night, the one when I panicked, but I wasn't panicking this time. The rush of adrenaline through my body was pleasure, excitement, at seeing his body rise up over mine.

The press of his cock deepened at the shift in position and I gasped, eyes fluttering. Snake kissed my neck, the curve of my breast, the hard peak of my nipple.

"God, I want you to fill me." The words came out unbidden as I spread my thighs wider. "I need you."

Snake chuffed, warm air fluttering over my face, but he complied with his hips, beginning a hard thrust that had me moaning and gasping.

Like a whore, a voice in my head whispered. I heard it, but I didn't acknowledge it. Couldn't acknowledge it because all my feelings, my emotions, my thoughts were tied up in the thrusting of Snake's body inside mine.

His cock pushed and thrust and moved inside me, hitting every tender, pleasurable spot of flesh.

Snake moved a hand between us and the pad of his thumb found my clit. It was enough, finally enough.

I screamed, the orgasm ripping through my body almost too much, an out-of-control inferno that threatened to burn me up.

I felt Snake's strained laugh against my throat, but he didn't stop moving his thumb or his body, pushing me deeper and deeper into my orgasm, until the sensation was almost painful. Until I almost wanted to squirm away from it because it was too much.

Snake's body pounded into mine a few more times as I clenched and broke around his cock.

"Shit," he growled against my neck. He slammed into me one final time and then his body went taut and his shoulders shook with the force of his own release.

His body went slack over me and we just breathed together for a moment, sweat-slicked skin stuck together.

Snake groaned, finally pulling free of my body, and rolling back on to his back. His hands trembled as he pulled the used condom off, tying off the end.

He got up and discarded it in the kitchen trash can. He looked practically radiant, wandering around naked in my apartment.

He rubbed a hand through his tousled hair. "Do you mind if I shower?" A quick grin. "Long day."

I was still naked on the bed and suddenly the awkwardness started to creep in because I was not sure what to do next.

"Um, sure, if you mind not having any hot water. I have to pee first."

I grabbed the throw blanket and wrapped it around me, scurrying off to the bathroom. I paused to wipe his cum off my chest with the edge of hand towel, watching the movement in the mirror with a tinge of regret. I didn't want to erase the memory of him.

We swapped places in the bathroom, still without much talking. Was that normal?

I pulled on some sweats and heard the shower come on as I curled up on the bed, still wrapped in my blanket. The bed smelled like us—like Snake's cologne and sex.

I heard a yelp and covered my smile with blanket.

It wasn't supposed to feel this good—sex outside of the marriage bed—that's what they all said. I had finally slid down the slippery slope, committed the great sin, and had thoroughly enjoyed myself while doing it. There was a clear demarcation in my head between what Hunter had done to me and what Snake and I had done together.

There was the age-old, familiar slither of shame up my spine, the one that my church community had cultivated so thoroughly.

But there was also a sense of freedom, a lightness in my chest.

I had actually *enjoyed* sex. With a man who didn't see my desires as an afterthought at best, or beside the point, at worst.

Snake finally emerged from the bathroom, just as my lids were beginning to droop. He was tightly wrapped in my teal and floral bathrobe, the hem just barely covering the curve of his ass. His hair was still damp.

"So, I forgot I don't have a change of clean clothes."

I grinned up at him, goofy, happy, sated. "Who cares?"

He grinned back, his dark brown eyes molten once again. He dropped the robe and climbed into bed with me, snuggling me firmly against his chest. He smelled like my peach body wash.

I sighed heavily, like I had just sunk into a hot bath. And it felt like that, being wrapped in his embrace.

His nose nuzzled against my hairline. "How are you feeling?"

"Are you looking for a report card?" I teased, running a finger through the soft hair on his sternum.

His fingers kneaded along my hips, my lower back. "Your scream was the only report card I needed."

"Oh, don't get so full of yourself yet. You promised to make me come so many times, I'd be begging you to stop. I haven't begged yet."

I was playing with fire; I knew that by the gleam in his eyes, the salacious curve of his lips, the firm grip of his hands.

He hummed, but there were dark circles forming on the soft skin under his eyes and I was barely stifling a yawn, even as I teased.

It had been a long damn day.

His thoughts seemed to be heading in the same direction, even as his hand slid down my sweatpants.

His other hand cradled the back of my head, tucking it under his chin. My breath hitched as his finger touched my pussy, finding my clit with ease.

He applied pressure quickly and confidently, our chests heaving together. My eyes closed, and I clung to his shoulders as I rode out another orgasm on his hand.

That was all it took.

I was asleep almost instantly, before the pulses had even finished with my body, curled against his chest with Snake's hand still in my pants.

Chapter Fifteen
DAMAGED GOODS

All my bravado from the night before faded away in the cold light of day.

I left Snake asleep in my bed and scurried out to work before the sun had even fully come up. I brushed and braided my hair in the car.

It may not have been the smartest move to leave a man I had only known for a few months alone inside my apartment. But it's not like I didn't also know where he lived if anything went missing. And besides, I didn't have anything worth stealing anyway unless you counted my crate of half-used oil paints.

Like a real coward, I sent him a text before he could text me.

Sorry. Had to work. Lock the handle if you have to leave, okay?

I probably could have thrown an emoji in there to soften the blow, but I couldn't think of a good one for the situation. Maybe I should have just thrown an octopus in there and left him guessing.

I was in the parking lot at work—I had some time to kill before my shift because I left way too early—finishing putting on a light coat of makeup when my phone started vibrating with an incoming call.

My heart dropped into my stomach, thinking that it might have been him, calling me. But a quick glance at the screen said *Grammy*.

I hadn't heard from Grammy, my maternal grandmother, in almost a year so it was curiosity that made me accept the call.

"Hey, Grammy," I said, clearing my throat.

"Hey, Honeybee, how are you?" The casual use of her nickname for me touched a deep-buried, broken part of my heart.

"I'm fine."

"We missed you at Thanksgiving."

My fingers flexed on the steering wheel. Grammy lived in Virginia, so I wasn't aware she had come into town for Thanksgiving. But, seeing as I had my mom's number blocked, she wouldn't have been able to tell me. I guessed Grammy didn't bother to reach out either. Not that I would have showed up anyway.

"Your mom misses you. She said you still won't talk to her."

I resisted the urge to say "no shit" to my eighty-year-old grandmother.

"Yeah, well. That kind of happens when you get kicked out of your home." I said it casually, but my stomach was in knots.

There was a deep silence on the other end of the line, as if she was weighing her next words carefully. "I think you should come back."

I frowned. "Come back where?"

"Come back to the church."

I barked out a disbelieving laugh. The audacity. There were just some people at some ages who you were not going to be able to change. "Are you serious right now?"

"Your mom says there's a new pastor. Young. Very progressive." There was a note of hopefulness in her voice, as if all it would take to bring me back was a young pastor.

"You forget I'm damaged goods, remember?" That was a phrase that got thrown around a lot in youth groups. Damaged goods. She kissed her boyfriend. Damaged goods. She led her boyfriend from the path of righteousness. Damaged goods. She's a sinner. Damaged goods. It's her fault, she shouldn't have worn that dress that was too short. Damaged goods.

There was more silence and then a brief sigh. "Honeybee. Jesus forgives all our sins."

"Did she tell you about the abortion?"

More pauses. "Yes. She did. You were just a baby."

"Seventeen." I pulled on a loose string on my jeans. "Not even a legal adult yet. Do you wanna know what she said to me when I told her?"

"Sheenah—"

"She called me a murderer. She told me I'd burn in hell for murdering my baby. And then she cried. She said that to her seventeen-year-old daughter." I took a breath. "You think I should forgive a church who taught my boyfriend it was okay if he sexually assaulted me? Do you think he asked for forgiveness for what he did?"

I was shaking now, regretting the words that came spewing out of my mouth but feeling relief at the same time, like draining an abscess.

Grammy probably didn't deserve my ire. But I wasn't talking to the person I wanted to rage at the most.

I remembered that day so vividly—I mean, how could you forget one of the days that changed your life forever?

It was cold for March, the temperature having randomly dropped after a few days of nice, balmy Kentucky springtime. I could wear a pair of black leggings and a baggy sweatshirt to hide my body.

I had driven to Chicago and back so I could get the abortion without notifying my parents, since I was a minor, under the pretense that I was spending the day with Hunter and his family.

He was a good, God-fearing boy and his parents were good, God-fearing people, so it wasn't something my mother questioned.

I knew something was wrong as soon as the flimsy screen door of our trailer slammed shut behind me. I was exhausted, wrung-dry and spit back out, bleeding. I just wanted to curl up on my tiny twin daybed, hide under the covers, and sleep for a hundred years.

But my mom was up waiting for me, sitting at our kitchen table, eyes red and face bloated.

She looked up at me and said, "Hunter hasn't seen you in a week." Her eyes were accusatory. Could she tell that I was minus the products of conception?

I just shrugged, figuring it would be better to keep my silence.

I tried to walk past her and to my room, but she grabbed my arm, her fingers like tiny vices. "What did you do?"

Her voice was low, hushed, like we were in a horror movie and if she spoke too loudly, whatever monster was hunting us would hear.

Like maybe *I* was the monster.

"Sheenah, I know if you talk to her, you'll feel better. I know she loves you."

I jumped, startled by Grammy's voice again in my ear. "Did she put you up to this?"

"No, I just thought—"

I couldn't take it anymore, so I hung up on her. The guilt of hanging up on my grandmother, the one I was closest to growing up, would probably haunt me, but I just couldn't take it anymore.

I tossed my phone into the passenger seat, feeling the familiar constriction in my chest. My hands shook but I braced them on the steering wheel. It was laughable that they thought I could just walk into another church, sit in front of another male pastor, and feel nothing other than dread or panic.

I heard my phone start vibrating again with another call from Grammy. This time I didn't answer and let it go to voicemail.

I took a deep breath, willing my pulse to slow and my body to still.

It was going to be a hellish shift.

I left work and trundled back home with anxiety churning in my stomach.

Snake had never responded to my text message and I didn't know how to feel about that. He had a right to be miffed that I ghosted him this morning, after what was, empirically, a good time.

He had a right to his feelings, but I also had a right to my own, which were currently a tangled, unreadable mess.

My apartment was locked and tidy when I entered. The bed had even been made, throw blanket spread out neatly again at the bottom.

I washed my hands real quick, changed, and then marched upstairs to apologize. I knew Snake was home because I saw his sleek SUV in the parking lot.

I knocked and his deep voice responded with, "Door's open."

Snake was standing bare-chested—Jesus, did the man own a damn shirt?—in front of the flower girl canvas he and I had worked on before.

Only a few weeks before. A month? Had it only been a month? It felt like he had been orbiting my life for a lot longer.

He had greatly expanded our painting.

She had a background now, a sprawling meadow landscape that weaved in and around her transparent torso.

I cleared my throat awkwardly. "She looks good. Do you have a name yet?"

He sighed, shoulders twitching. He put his brush and palette down on the farmhouse bench and turned to stare at me, still silently.

There was something wary, maybe even hurt, in his eyes, in the stillness of his body.

I rubbed my sweaty palms on my jeans. "Look, I'm sorry—"

"You could have told me we were just doing the bump-and-run. That way I could know what to expect."

Pissed, definitely pissed. "I shouldn't...I shouldn't have left...like that." I may have my own trauma, my own shitload of baggage, but that still didn't give me the right to treat other people badly. Especially people, especially Snake, who had been nothing other than good to me.

He arched an eyebrow, as if expecting me to continue and try to explain myself.

I looked down at my feet as they shuffled. "I'm not any good at this. I don't know how to do this."

"Do what?"

With great effort, I pulled my gaze back up to catch his dark eyes. "Be with someone else."

Like opposite poles of two magnets, we walked towards each other until our chests touched.

His lips crashed against mine, hands roughly dragging my body up against his.

We fucked on the farmhouse bench.

Snake let me down gently on his cock, so slowly that I felt every second of stretch. So slowly, my thighs and arms quivered with anticipation.

I clung to his shoulders, eyes closed, breaths mingling, as he fucked up into me. The slow slide of his cock had me gasping for air.

It was a funny thing, to have your childhood belief system debunked, to have it shatter to pieces, born away by each wave of pleasure that wracked my body.

Pleasure I wasn't supposed to have, pleasure that I wasn't supposed to want.

Snake grabbed a handful of my hair, tugging my head back as he increased the speed of his thrusts. I moaned again as my throat was bared to him. His hot mouth kissed and sucked on the delicate skin of my neck. He nipped gently and my body shook as I came apart on his cock.

Fucking Snake was almost spiritual; a balm on my lonely soul.

CHAPTER SIXTEEN

SOMETHING A MAN WOULD DO

Once we'd finished, discarded the used condom, and cleaned up, I realized I needed to leave...again. I pulled up my pants, red-cheeked.

"So, um, I really don't want to say this, but I need to go do homework."

Despite my best efforts—okay, so maybe it wasn't my very best effort—I had indeed put Howard's term paper off until the last minute. I had collected everything I needed in terms of resources, but now I had to piece it all together and string it along with my "mediocre" thesis statement.

Snake pulled on his own sweats, the soft gray material sliding up and over his sculpted hips. "Go get it."

"What?"

"Go get your stuff. I'll make you a sandwich."

I was so shell-shocked I could only walk down to my apartment in a daze, mouth slightly agape, gather my books, laptop, and charger, and then wander back upstairs.

Snake had indeed whipped me up a sandwich which was stacked neatly on a paper plate next to a pile of Cheetos.

Snake had the Cheetos bag and was eating them while leaning up against the sink.

"I didn't know what kind of toppings you liked so I left it naked." He wiggled his eyebrows suggestively.

I laughed as I put my stuff down on the end of his bed. "Naked is fine."

The sandwich was simple: ham and cheese on white bread. But, somehow, it tasted like the best cold ham and cheese sandwich I had ever eaten.

An odd feeling squeezed around my heart.

I was feeling sentimental over a sandwich.

It may have also been the way Snake's eyes watched my mouth as I ate. And my fingers as I licked Cheeto dust off them.

People didn't make food for me.

I ate frozen meals in less than five minutes or scrounged up bits and bobs from the infrequent trips I made to the grocery.

We ate quickly in companionable silence and then I went and posted up on his bed, while Snake resumed his position in front of his work in progress.

He chuckled. "My paint is dry."

My face flushed, remembering the reason for his dry paint. I opened my laptop to my document and notes pages, while Snake redid his palette, humming softly under his breath.

I wondered briefly if he would get upset if I put earbuds in, but he seemed happy enough in front of his canvas so I snuck one in.

I clicked around, tip-typing on my keyboard, until I had pounded out a halfway decent introductory paragraph.

"What do you know about Sylvia Plath and confessional poetry?" I mused aloud, but it was still mostly a rhetorical question.

He paused, tapping the end of a paintbrush against his chin. "Not a damn thing."

"Really?"

"Really, college girl."

I held up one of the books I'd checked out from the library for research. "She's really good. You should try reading some of her stuff some time. I just wish I didn't have to write about it."

"What's your essay about?"

"Oh, you know, the classic struggle between domesticity and art. Plath seemed to be one of those reluctant wives and mothers. Her writing is filled with anxiety and despair over having to choose."

He made a few strokes with the brush. "Which poems are you using to support that?"

"I've narrowed it down to a few. I like 'Mirror,' and 'Three Women,' and 'Edge.'"

Snake might profess to know nothing about Sylvia Plath, but he knew art and he knew how to analyze and dissect it. He knew symbolism and theme.

We discussed the evidence I'd be pulling from the text, which lines would support my interpretation and my reading of the poems. Snake was astute and wouldn't let me get away with half-assery. I took feverish notes as we talked, the outline of my paper slowly forming and growing.

"I would also like to include biographical information, because I think that's important to understanding her work. I think sometimes people don't realize how young she was."

"How young?"

"She was only thirty when she died."

Snake paused, paintbrush held aloft. "Oh, wow. That is young."

"And there's some controversy surrounding her posthumous work. There're some rumors that her husband was abusive and that he got rid of some of her journals and work that talked about the abuse."

We both stilled.

I pretended to be suddenly very interested in one of the books I'd brought, face flushing with heat. I hadn't meant to bring down the mood by bringing the topic back to both our traumas.

But Snake shook it off, shoulders visibly relaxing as he went back to his painting. "Sounds like something a man would do."

I snorted, relieved that we could pick back up where we left off. I closed the book and my laptop screen, settling both in my lap to look at him.

His profile was limned in the soft light of his apartment, brow creased slightly with concentration. His hand moved confidently over the canvas.

"Can I ask you a completely personal and off-topic question?"

Snake arched a brow. "I guess." He put his brush down. "Should I be nervous?"

I shrugged. "I mean, not really."

He crossed his arms over his chest, biceps straining. "Okay, shoot."

I let out a soft exhale. "Do you believe in God?"

He blinked a few times, as if he wasn't quite sure he had under-stood me correctly. Then he cocked his head, a pensive look on his face. "I'm not really religious, if that's what you mean."

"No, like, do you believe in God, capital G."

He sighed, coming to flop down on the bed beside me. "I didn't prepare my theology notes." He grinned up at me, hand going to rest warmly on my knee. "Honestly? I'm not sure. I wasn't raised religious. My dad didn't have time for anything other than booze, you know? But I think there's something bigger than us out there. I'm just not sure what it is. Could be God, could be a god, could be gods."

I arched a brow. "Could be a goddess."

His mouth quirked. "Could be. Sometimes I wondered if there really is a God, how could He let my dad treat my mom the way he did? How could He let my mom stay?"

I nodded. The sentiment was a familiar one. How could He let bad things happen to good people?

"Why do you ask?"

I shrugged again, picking at a loose thread on the hem of my sweats. "I was raised evangelical. You know the kind. White, loud." I gave him a meaningful look. "They used God as an excuse for a lot of things."

"So, do *you* believe in God?"

"I don't know. I stopped believing in organized religion. But organized religion and God are not the same things."

Gah, my grandmother's call earlier must have really done a num-ber on my psyche. I hadn't wrestled with the idea of God or no God in a long time. It was a battle I had fought after Hunter, after the abortion, but was something I had left behind, put on the back burner, to be dealt with later, whenever later was. I guessed later turned out to be now.

"You don't have to be religious to believe in something bigger than yourself." He gently squeezed my knee.

I smiled softly at him, twining my fingers through his.

Even growing up, I had never been the typical church youth group girlie. I think there was always this little voice in the back of my head that would perk up and mutter, "something about this isn't right."

I had doubts.

Maybe that's what made me finally walk away from Hunter. I finally had enough and I was finally listening to that little doubting voice.

"I went no contact with God when I went no contact with my parents, after the abortion."

The words left my mouth in a quick rush. I hadn't really meant to share that with Snake; I hadn't decided if I wanted to tell him about the abortion at all. But a part of me was just ready to finally let everything go, let all the secrets out and stop holding everything inside my brain and then feel guilty about it.

Snake just raised his eyebrows, his expression otherwise neutral. "Okay. Shit happens."

I let out a breath, glancing away from him.

"Were you expecting me to judge you for that?"

Was I? Did I finally spill that dirty little secret because I was hoping it would drive a wedge between us? To finally make him see what kind of person I am? To make him walk away before either of us got too invested?

I flopped my arms in a poor imitation of a shrug before I realized he was still holding my hand. My chest constricted.

I wrapped his hand in both of mine, rubbing my thumb across the inked Medusa on the back of his hand.

Snake was a man who knew violence, who probably knew desperation. And I felt safe with him. And for some reason, I always had.

"I begged him not to tell our parents and he did it anyway. I was desperately, invisibly miserable for weeks. And either no one noticed or no one cared. And that's when I knew I wouldn't survive that. So I chose myself."

Snake's face was soft, liquid brown eyes big and solemn. His fingers flexed in mine. "Can I tell you a secret?"

I huffed out a breath. "I mean, I've told you all mine."

"Sometimes"—he took a breath—"sometimes, I think my mom would have left my dad, if I wasn't around."

I frowned. "Isaac."

He gave me a tight-lipped smile. "What? It's true. I was able to make something of myself in spite of him, but it's something I thought about a lot. Especially when I was growing up. Could my mom have walked away if I wasn't there? Maybe. I mean, I'll never really know, but maybe." He took another deep breath, eyes never leaving my face. "What I'm trying to say is that it's okay that you saved yourself."

I glanced away again, not courageous enough to keep his gaze. And I felt the hot burn of unshed tears pressing against my eyes and I didn't want to cry in front of him again.

My throat constricted with the effort of keeping the tears at bay. I tried to focus on the canvas that Snake had been working on, but the colors were all blurring together.

"I bet no one's ever told you that," he said.

I barked out a clipped laugh, not because anything was funny, but because my body had to release the tension somehow. "You'd win. I've been told a lot of things, but not that."

He made that deep humming sound in his throat that always seemed to send heat straight to my belly.

I leaned down and put my laptop and books on the floor and then wriggled around until Snake and I were nose to nose on the bed.

I put my palm on his cheek, his light stubble rasping across my skin. "We're a mess."

"Yeah, but we're cute."

I laughed, for real this time, grateful for his levity. I brushed my thumb across the tender skin under his eye. "Thank you."

His brows rose. "For what?"

I bit my lip, pretending to think. "Um, for the mind-blowingly good sex, obviously."

He arched against me like a cat. "Ah, yes, I will collect my accolades now."

I giggled and Snake gathered me against his chest so that my nose was buried in the hollow of his throat. It required some readjusting of our positions since we were the same height. He threw a leg over my hip.

"I was being serious, though, about the thank you."

"I know you were." He kissed the top of my head.

Chapter Seventeen
PRETTY GIRL

To add insult to injury, Dr. Howard had decreed that we all would be doing a final presentation on our term paper topics. And—this was emphasized with a short finger in the air—it better not just be a verbatim repeat of our papers.

He would know.

He'd made this pronouncement at our penultimate class meeting of the semester. There was much grumbling as we left the classroom, but I honestly couldn't care less. I loved putting together a good PowerPoint; that would be a breeze compared to the actual writing of the final paper.

And I didn't mind spending our last class period listening to other presentations.

I left Howard's class feeling remarkably light for once. I had already turned in my final paper days ago via the learning management system so Howard could run it through the plagiarism checker. After talking it through with Snake, I felt remarkably confident about my paper. I felt confident that it at least made sense and my thesis was properly defended, even if Howard couldn't deign to agree with me.

Rayme looped their arm through my elbow as we walked down the hallway. They were practically skipping.

"Only one more week, eh."

I grinned. "Finally."

"I wasn't going to make it much longer."

"Oh, me neither."

"We're definitely getting drunk when the semester ends."

Before I could respond, Dr. Howard's sharp voice stopped us both in our tracks.

"Ms. Green-Barnes. Could I see you in my office?"

Rayme's eyebrows shot up and I'm sure the panicked look on their face mirrored my own. They mouthed *good luck* before leaving me alone in the hallway.

I almost glanced at my wrist, but I didn't wear a watch. "It's late."

Howard brushed past me, a leather folio tucked under his arm like an expensive accessory. "I know. It won't take much of your time."

He kept walking, but I dithered in the hallway.

It was after nine o'clock at night. Yeah, our class just ended but it was still late. I'd never seen him ask to see anyone else after class. Was that weird? Was he weird? Was Dr. Howard about to reveal himself as a creep that preyed on college girls?

I checked my phone and already had a text from Rayme.

Text me when you're done and let me know

you're still alive. Or if we need to make
a title 9 complaint about dr. dickhead.

I sent them back a thumbs-up emoji and then followed behind Howard at a safe distance.

It was not a long walk to the office building; Howard was already behind his assigned desk, shuffling around and clicking on the keyboard when I resignedly entered the room.

My anxiety spiked almost immediately, remembering the last time I was in this office with him.

I stood by the door until he looked up.

"You can sit down." There was a small furrow between his brows.

That could not be a good sign. I did not want this meeting to last long enough that I had to be seated.

I inhaled deeply through my nose to head off the sudden racing of my heart and landed heavily in one of the plastic chairs in front of the desk.

Dr. Howard faced me, steepling his fingers in front of his face in what I'm sure he thought was a pensive gesture. It just made him look like a pompous dick.

We stared at each other.

"Sheenah," he started. "I know I was hard on you the last time we spoke, but I'm only hard on you because I want you to perform your best."

Jesus fuck. We needed to have this conversation after nine o'clock at night? I was fucking tired. I had gone into work early so that I could make sure I left in order to get to his class on time. But heaven forbid I tell him that.

"Um, okay?"

"I want you to be successful, but I didn't expect you to resort to desperate measures in order to do so."

I rubbed my sweaty palms on my jeans. "What are you talking about?"

He sighed. "I think you know."

I bit my tongue to stop the first thing that came to mind from slipping out of my mouth because it would not be pleasant.

"Dr. Howard, can you elaborate? I don't know what you're talking about."

He turned his gaze to whatever was on the computer screen. "I had the chance to read your essay. It was really quite accomplished."

That was supposed to be good news, right? "Okay, thanks. I appreciate that."

"Yes, well, did you write it?"

My heart stuttered in my chest and it took my brain a couple seconds to process what he said. I blinked owlishly. "Excuse me?"

"I said, did you write—"

"Of course I did."

"It's significantly more developed than your other work for our class. Almost on a different level entirely."

I pointed an accusatory finger at the computer. "Did it get flagged for plagiarism?"

"Well, no."

"Did I cite any of my sources incorrectly?"

His frown deepened. "Save for a few misplaced commas in the notations, which I have marked, no."

I could feel the flush starting in my face and traveling down my neck, but I wasn't going to back down, not now. Not when we only had a week left of the semester. Not when I was so close to getting what I wanted. "So what exactly are you accusing me of, Dr. Howard?"

He scrubbed his hands across his face, as if I was being the most difficult, obtuse person in the entire world.

"Ms. Green-Barnes. I have spent almost sixteen weeks grading and reading your written work. And this final essay is leagues better than your previous work. So, I don't believe you are the original author of this essay."

That was sure a lot of words for "I think you're a liar and a cheat."

"Are you kidding me right now?"

"I most certainly am not. Academic dishonesty is taken very seriously."

My hands clenched violently in my jeans. "I wrote every word of that damn essay."

"Now, Ms. Green-Barnes, there's no need for hostility."

"Did it ever occur to you that students can improve their writing over a course? Like, they're actually learning something and you're actually teaching something? Isn't that literally your job?"

The words came spewing out of my mouth like vomit, and it was Howard's turn to blink incredulously at me. Like the thought of teaching had never even crossed his mind. I wasn't going to let him fail me without a fight. And I wasn't going to mention that I had spent more time on this final essay than all the other written assignments combined. Some things were just better left unknown.

I stood up, hoisting my backpack. "I wrote every single word of that essay, Dr. Howard."

"Ms. Green-Barnes, please—"

"And you have no proof otherwise. If you fail me, I will be going to talk to the Dean. And the Provost, and probably the Title IX Coordinator with *my* evidence."

His usual smooth, tan complexion paled at the mention of Title IX.

I didn't wait for a further response.

I left the communal office, letting the heavy door slam closed on my way out.

I sobbed on the way home, hand quivering on the gear shift of my old Honda.

It felt good threatening Dr. Howard in the moment, but now I was terrified of the repercussions. Other than the running list of sexist and misogynist comments that he'd made over the course of the semester—which Rayme was keeping in their notes app—I didn't have any evidence of anything.

And I'm pretty sure universities didn't punish professors for being sexist. I'm sure Rayme would let me borrow the list if I needed to, but what would it prove?

I had texted them before I started driving home that I was okay and unharmed.

What did he want?

> *He thinks I plagiarized*
> *the final paper.*

WHAT AN ASS.
…you didn't,
tho, right?

> *I didn't.*

Eh, don't worry about
him. Dr. Dickhead is just
on a short white man power trip.

I needed a Literature class to meet graduation requirements. I had to have one, whether it was Dr. Dickhead's or another one. If he failed me, it would ding my GPA and I'd have to retake it or something else.

I had already set up my final semester with an easy twelve hours of studio classes. If I had to deal with Dr. Howard *again*, I didn't know if I would make it. No matter what I said, no matter what I did or how hard I worked, he was bound and determined to see me as just dumb white trash. And I couldn't go through another whole semester trying to prove him wrong.

Snake was working at the shop tonight, so he wouldn't be home until one or two in the morning.

I spent a little time freshening up and then put on some cooling under eye masks to try to reduce the damage to my face incurred by my crying spree in the car.

I must have dozed off, because I woke up to Snake climbing into the bed with me, the heat from his body sinking deep into my skin. My heart lurched for just a second, but I recognized his smell, the calluses on his hands, and remembered that I'd left the door unlocked for him.

I didn't usually leave my door unlocked for men to drop by, but Snake told me he would come over after work so I was expecting him.

Snake's body curled around mine.

The easy, familiar domesticity was absolutely terrifying, but I couldn't help myself. Couldn't help how much I desperately wanted him and the slow, tender relationship that was blooming.

One of his fingers poked at one of the masks that were still attached to my face. "This is sexy."

I gave a sleepy laugh. "Oh, shut up."

His nose nuzzled my ear. "How was your day?"

My heart lurched again, for an entirely different reason this time. "My professor thinks I plagiarized my Sylvia Plath essay."

"Are you fucking serious?" He sounded affronted, like he had a personal stake in my grade. Which, granted, he had helped me iron out some ideas.

I tugged on his forearm to bring him closer to my body again. "It's whatever. I told him I didn't, so I guess we'll see if he believes me or not."

"That's such bullshit," he said, but settled back down behind me in our spoon, large hand palming my belly. "Do you need this class?"

"Unfortunately, yes."

"See, this is why I didn't go to college."

I laughed again. "It hasn't really been all bad. The professor is a misogynist, but I've actually really enjoyed the readings. I might keep our textbook. Although"—I pinched him playfully on the arm—"I might need to resell it to pay my tattoo artist."

He laughed, a rumbling, deep sound that brushed air across my neck. "You're just now worried about paying me?"

"Well, we kind of started having sex like right after, so I figured...quid pro quo."

I was only wearing underwear and a thin tank top, and his warm hand slid under the waistband of my underwear. I was sure he could probably feel my raised nipples through the thin fabric of my tank.

"Quid pro quo, eh." His fingers traveled lower. "Call us even. I squared it away with Austin since he owed me one."

His fingers ghosted over my mound and I squirmed, all thoughts of tiredness, tattoos, and GPAs disappearing from my immediate thoughts.

"Oh, I almost forgot. I have good news for you." His fingers stopped and I whined with pent-up frustration.

"This better be *very* good news," I ground out, pushing my hips back against his.

"Niyah will be emailing you, but you sold two paintings."

I stopped moving abruptly, tilting my head to look over my shoulder to try to catch his eyes. "Are you serious?"

He tweaked a nipple through my shirt. "Why do you sound surprised? Your work is good."

"Yeah, but 'can pass art class' good and 'people will pay their hard-earned money to hang this on their wall' good are two entirely different things."

"I guess you're in the second category now."

His good news delivered, Snake pressed his warm mouth to my throat, hand absently playing with my nipple. But I was distracted. I had sold not one, but *two*, original paintings. I had earned money from my art. People wanted it. People paid for it. People had paid *hundreds* for it.

"Earth to Sheenah." Snake's fingers slipped across my clit. "I'm going to finger fuck you now."

I flushed and grinned, back arching as he rubbed down firmly on the sensitive bud. "Oh, by all means—" I gasped as two fingers delved up inside me. "Be my guest."

He hummed, the sound vibrating against my throat and sending warmth coursing through my limbs. He knew my body so well by now—dare I say, even better than I did—and I was orgasming under his fingers in less than a minute.

I felt the wetness on his fingers as he worked my panties down my legs.

"Something about those little masks just gets me going."

I laughed, the sound coming out unexpectedly loud in the quiet apartment.

"You laugh now," he growled.

But I was all serious again when he pulled one of my legs up; I could feel the hard press of his cock against my ass.

His fingers gripped my thigh, pulling my leg farther away from my body so that my pussy was open and exposed. My heart thudded in my chest, pulse pounding in my ears. I reached back, hand grabbing the back of Snake's head, grip pulling his mouth even tighter to me.

The head of his cock pressed against my opening.

"Fuck me, Isaac, fuck me—" I keened as one hard thrust sheathed him entirely inside my body. I wanted to buck, but he held me still, pussy quivering softly over his cock.

"Say it again," he growled against the shell of my ear.

"Fuck me, Isaac." I had wanted the words to come out as a demand, but they fell from my lips like a plea.

His hips started to undulate, the strokes firm but shallow. From our position, the angle wasn't deep, but it was slow and steady, the pressure building in my core at the same pace.

He peppered kisses down my throat, his free hand playing leisurely with my nipple.

The tenderness of it all was driving me insane. I writhed and pushed my hips back, trying to take him deeper, to *force* him deeper.

His chuckle brushed across my skin. "Take it. Take your pleasure from me, pretty girl."

I made a strangled sound and then brought my own fingers to my clit. His hips popped and my fingers rubbed furiously until I was breaking and fluttering against his hard cock and coming with a long, high-pitched moan.

Snake's own orgasm chased my own; he thrust into me until we were both spent and shaking and pulling in long breaths.

He rolled over onto his back, cock pulling reluctantly free of my body. "Damn." His chest was still heaving.

I turned over and swatted his straining abdomen. "You're such a tease."

He grinned up at me, eyes pleasure-heavy. "I like to see you touch yourself."

"Mm-hmm."

I rolled the condom off him, Snake's eyes watching my every move, and took it to the bathroom to clean up.

I was washing my hot cheeks off with cool water from the sink when I noticed the purple-blue mark on my neck.

I screamed.

I came back in the room and Snake was already half off the bed, eyes panicked. "What is it?"

I was practically shaking. I pointed an angry finger at my neck. "You gave me a hickey!"

Snake momentarily froze and then his shoulders started shaking with barely contained laughter. He covered his face with both hands and fell back on the bed.

"This isn't funny!"

Snake had a hand on his stomach, like he could barely contain himself. "I'm sorry. It's not-not funny."

His hysterics would beg to differ.

But he was still apologizing. "I really am sorry. I didn't mean to do that. I haven't given a girl a hickey since, like, seventh grade."

My eyes widened. "Seventh grade!"

I crossed my arms angrily and waited for him to get control of himself.

Snake sat up on the bed, thick legs dangling off the side, hands crossed contritely over his crotch. Then he grinned at me like a goofy boy. "It was an accident, I swear."

I went and sat down beside him, arms still crossed. He nuzzled me on the shoulder and I couldn't help the grin that spread across my own face.

I shoved his hard bicep. "I'm mad at you. I'm going to have to wear a scarf."

He continued his contrite nuzzling. "It's winter."

I swatted at him, but he just wrapped his arms around me and tackled me to the bed, curling all his hot limbs around mine.

"People are going to notice."

He buried his face in my neck. "What are people going to notice?"

That I'm yours.

The words almost slipped right out of my mouth. They were there, on the tip of my tongue, ready to return his jest. But would it be a joke?

I wrapped my arms around his broad shoulders, nose in his hair, inhaling that delicious scent that was all too familiar to me now.

This was getting too dangerous; we were too close. Snake was too close and I was enjoying it too much.

Snake had told me that it was okay that I had chosen myself. What would he say if he knew that I planned to continue choosing myself, over and over and over again?

Chapter Eighteen

ISAAC

A week and half later I was hanging out with Snake at Sabbath Ink, drawing and sketching while he worked. Because that was apparently something we did now. I was dolled up more than usual, in a slouchy jersey dress that had a deep scoop neck with my hair in soft waves down my back. The effort put into the waves was worth it when Snake saw me in the dress, his gaze heating immediately, a matching flush spreading across the exposed skin of my chest.

The shop was apparently super casual, and it wasn't unusual to have people just hanging around like me, most of them other tattoo artists, but still my presence wasn't so out of the ordinary for the other artists or clients to take note.

It was actually really interesting to watch Snake work. He would explain things to me: why he chose the different needles, why he was shading a piece a certain way. I'm sure his clients thought I was in training or something as I listened avidly with my sketchbook propped on my knees.

What I was actually working on were some new designs for my shop. With the semester over, I had about a month to devote solely to my brand and crank out some new material before the final semester of my college career started. I wanted this winter collection to be fun and flirty, with some unique silhouettes. I might even consider breaking out some floral patterns or creating my own.

I drew absently in my sketchbook while Snake readied his last client of the night: a fresh-faced eighteen-year-old who was here for her birthday, along with a gaggle of her friends. They filled the shop with "oohs" and "ahhs" and high-pitched giggles and "oh my gods" so my presence definitely wasn't being noted.

"Can I have that instead?"

I looked up from my sketch to notice the girl standing next to the padded chair, pointing at me. No, not at me, at what I was working on. A surrealist lady face with peonies for eyes.

Snake was sanitizing the chair, but raised his eyebrows.

"Um, what?" I said.

The girl gestured to my drawing emphatically. "That. I want that instead." She looked at Snake, blue eyes big and pleading and I knew it was an expression that usually got her what she wanted.

Snake's eyebrows shot up further into his hairline as he looked at me...and then he grinned. "Well, Sheenah, make the stencil."

The girl squealed and I grinned right back at him; I just couldn't help myself.

I finalized the drawing for the girl so that she could approve it before I made the stencil, Snake watching us with an amused expression on his face.

She then showed it to her entourage who all squealed very similarly while I flushed with pleasure at their enthusiasm.

Snake had to walk me to the printer area where the iPads were so that we could recreate my design digitally for the stencils.

Our shoulders brushed as he bent over the iPad.

"Are you sure this is okay?" I whispered, leaning close to his ear.

"If the client is happy, I'm happy." His mouth quirked in a wry grin. "It's leagues better than the butterfly she had me draw."

"You're not offended?"

He pressed his hip into mine. "Never. You better be careful before I put you to work drawing all my designs." He gave me a wink as he walked off to show the girl the digital version of her design for the next round of approvals.

The girl was even more pleased with her design in digital format, so the tattooing commenced, the girl not even flinching when Snake pressed the needle to her forearm.

We were about two hours into the tattoo—and I was five winter season designs deep—when Niyah approached, her sky-high stilettos clacking along the tiled floor.

She stopped in front of Snake's station and all our heads swiveled to look at her, except Snake, who kept his eyes on his work, swiping a paper towel across the ink and blood welling on the girl's arm.

"Snake, your mom's here."

I stopped breathing.

Niyah's eyes were hard, her hot pink lips pursed, as she stared down at Snake and I wondered how much she knew about his parents and his childhood.

Snake didn't look up but his body had stilled, the tattoo gun buzzing but no longer gliding across his client's skin.

I saw his nostrils flare. "I'm with a client."

Niyah put her hands on her hips. "I told her that."

He took a deep breath that made his chest move. "Just her?"

"She's the only one I saw. I didn't see anyone else with her."

Snake seemed to physically shake off the distraction, returning needle to skin. "I'm with a client. She can leave or she can wait."

Then he was in the zone again, without ever having raised his head.

Niyah looked like she was about to argue. She glanced at the door, long, beaded earrings swinging, before glancing back at Snake who was very studiously ignoring her.

Then she sighed and spun on one of her precariously high heels before stalking back to the front.

I leaned over in my chair, eyes following her to see if I could get a glimpse of the woman who was waiting on Snake. But the only thing I could see was the very large reception desk. Maybe she left? She wouldn't wait until Snake was finished. Would she?

Snake seemed to have shaken off the interruption, hand pulling fluid lines across skin once again, chatting genially with the girl and her friends.

I, however, was terribly distracted, my sketches abandoned as I watched Snake work like a professional.

I wanted him to look at me. I wanted to catch his gaze and see what was there, the pain and concern that he was hiding. I had heard it in his voice, in the stillness of his body. A fight or flight or freeze response.

But he seemed just as determined not to meet my gaze as he was determined to act like nothing had just happened.

From our previous conversations about his parents, I got the distinct impression that he didn't see them much and preferred it that way. So what was his mother doing here? How did she even know where he worked or where to find him?

Was his dad here too?

The thought sent my heart racing and I had to clench my fist to stop my hand from shaking.

Snake was going to finish his work.

Surely, she wouldn't wait that long?

Another two hours went by and Niyah's interruption was almost gone from my mind, lured into safety by the whirr of the machine and the friendly chatter of the girl's friends who cooed over my designs and took business cards and followed me on Instagram right then and there.

Snake sanitized and wrapped the new ink and provided the aftercare pamphlet and then the girl threw her arms around his neck and thanked him profusely while his cheeks pinked adorably.

A sliver of jealousy went through me but then she turned to me and did the same thing, her magnolia perfume filling my nose.

While Snake went to tidy up his station before we left for the night, I decided to take a peek at my final grades for the semester. They were due yesterday and should be posted by now.

I logged into my student portal, my breath stuck in my throat as I navigated to the final grades screen.

ENGL 3504 Contemporary Women Poets: Literature - C

My breath left me in a rush, shoulders visibly sagging. Dr. Dickhead had passed me in what was no less than a miracle. I had straight As in every other course for the semester, so the C felt especially grating, but that feeling was brief and overshadowed by relief.

I was done.

I was done with Dr. Howard and his class.

I never had to see that man again or defend myself or my opinions or listen to him opine about how much he didn't understand women.

I could have cried happy tears.

Snake was at my shoulder with a concerned expression on his face. "What's wrong?"

I tilted my phone in his direction. "I passed."

An undiluted grin broke across his face.

He clasped the back of my neck and kissed my forehead. "Let's go. I'll buy you a treat."

I perked up, stowing my phone back in my bag. "What kind of treat?"

Snake slung his own cute little messenger bag across his shoulder and then tucked my hand into the crook of his elbow. "Whatever you want."

I couldn't wipe the pleased, triumphant grin off my own face as we walked arm in arm out of the shop, past his coworkers and clients, waving goodbye to Niyah on the way out.

I had my doubts. About us, about our relationship, about his intentions, about my intentions. But I had doubts about literally everything in my life. I second-guessed almost every decision I had ever made. But Snake was fun and he was sweet and he was easy to be around. I felt like I could finally breathe.

We exited the shop laughing, our breaths misting in the chill December air. The night was perfect: clear, crisp, and glittery, Christmas lights twinkling on all the buildings.

And then a small voice said, "Isaac?"

We both whipped around at the same time, Snake almost taking me to the ground with the force of his turn—since I was still attached to his arm.

A small woman stood up from one of the benches out in front of the shop. She was short and thin, but her overall presence just seemed small. Her shoulders hunched, gloved hands picking at the front of her black parka.

Her skin was pale, and I thought I saw the outline of a blue bruise along the bottom of her jaw.

My heart lurched.

She had Snake's eyes, but while Snake's were lively, hers were a dull, muted, deep brown.

I felt Snake's tension through my hold on his arm. His shoulders stiffened and I felt his muscles hardening like someone had filled his body with lead.

"Isaac," she said again, fingers twitching.

"Mom." Snake's eyes darted around and I assumed he was looking to see if anyone else was with her. Like his dad. "What are you doing here?"

"I...we need to talk."

"Look, I don't have that much cash on me but I can go to the ATM real quick and get more. How much do you need?" Snake's words crashed out in a rush.

She held her hands up as if in defense. "I don't...it's not about money. We just...is there somewhere we can talk?"

It was already past ten so the only place open was the diner.

Snake's mom rode with us in his car.

I was too much of a chickenshit to ask him to take me home first, so I was just along for the most awkward car ride of my entire life.

We walked in and I didn't see anyone I knew, which I was so thankful for, I almost started praying again. I wasn't sure how *that* conversation would go.

Snake and I sat on the side of the booth opposite his mom, who looked around the diner like she'd never seen one before. Or maybe that was just how she normally looked with her too wide, dull eyes.

She ordered coffee, Snake ordered a latte, and I ordered chocolate milk.

"Isaac, are you going to introduce your friend?"

Snake looked startled, as if it just occurred that I was still with him and now he had to explain my presence to his mom.

So, I saved him. "Sheenah, ma'am."

She smiled sadly at me. "What a doll. You're so polite." She looked back at Snake. "And pretty too. Isaac, isn't she pretty?"

I wanted to disappear into the cracked plastic seat. I was going to have to change my name and flee the state after this interaction.

Thankfully, Snake finally decided to re-engage. "Who told you where I worked?"

"Don't you think I have a right to know where my son works?" For the first time, there was a bit of fire behind her words. A bit of anger in the tilt of her mouth.

"No. I don't."

Our drinks were delivered and I reached gratefully for my glass, giving the swirling light brown liquid my full attention.

She sighed. "Austin told me."

"I don't want you talking to my friends."

"Well, you won't talk to me. I needed to find you. If you hadn't changed your phone number, I wouldn't have had to track you down, would I?"

"You know why I changed my number."

I stared so hard into the depths of my cup I went cross-eyed. I definitely did not need to be present for whatever this was.

Another heavy sigh from his mom and the scrape of ceramic over the top of the table as she gripped her cup.

"I told you it was him or me and you chose him. You did. You made that choice, Mom." His voice was low but sharp and angry and I felt every word like a shard in my skin.

I'm sure his mom felt them much worse.

"I don't want to fight." Her voice was quiet, barely audible over the cacophony of the diner.

"Then tell me what you want so I can go home."

More scraping of her coffee cup. "It's your dad...he's sick, Isaac."

"How sick?"

"Stage four liver cancer."

Snake barked out a humorless laugh that was so sudden I jumped.

"Well, isn't that just ironic."

I finally glanced back up at his face. His voice was so cold, so sharp. His mouth was turned in an ugly grimace, warm eyes hard and mean. It wasn't an expression I'd ever seen on his face.

"Isaac," his mom chided. "He's still your father. And he's dying."

"Good." Snake slapped some bills on the table. "Sheenah, we're done."

He slid out of the booth without a backward glance and I scrambled to get up after him or be left behind. His mom was frowning but she didn't look otherwise surprised that he was leaving.

I felt like I should say something to her, but what. Nothing particularly useful came to mind, so I just followed Snake.

He was halfway across the parking lot. I had to jog to catch him.

"Snake, wait." I tugged on the sleeve of his jacket. "She's your mom, shouldn't we—"

He rounded on me with that angry look still on his face and I stopped in my tracks.

"No. You don't know what it was like. Growing up in that house."

"But, she—"

His hand came up and I flinched. I couldn't help it. The reaction was ingrained in my body. He was just gesticulating, I *knew* that, and my body flinched away from him anyway.

The emotion and the color immediately drained from his face, his eyes glancing at the hand that was frozen halfway in midair.

"Sheenah..." My name came out a strangled whisper. "I didn't—" His gaze caught on something behind me and his mouth went slack.

The change was so sudden, I whirled around. There was a man standing next to the door of the diner, standing next to Snake's mom, who had come out, zipped up in her parka again, small again, standing in his shadow.

They always look so ordinary, the abusers. It's almost unfair. You want them to look the part. You want them to look horrible, to look scary, to strike fear into the heart. Maybe that way you could avoid them.

Snake's dad looked so ordinary. He was lanky, with thin shoulders, salt-and-pepper hair that was thinning around the top, with grease stains on his canvas jacket.

An ordinary, working man.

Who hit his wife. Who would have hit his child.

"Isaac," he said, and his voice rumbled like a thunderstorm, like a hurricane, like the fall of an avalanche that would bury you.

Snake's whole body radiated fury, hands clenched into tight fists at his sides.

He moved to stalk past me, but I grabbed his arm with both hands like my life depended on it. I expected more resistance but he stopped fairly easily.

He pointed at his dad. "I hope you rot in hell."

His dad didn't flinch at the angry words, his face didn't so much as twitch. He just inclined his chin slightly, like he expected nothing less from Snake.

There was tension on the arm I held in my death-grip, like Snake wanted to move forward, like the non-reaction from his dad wasn't enough.

He took a step and I yanked. "Snake, no."

There was finally a reaction from his dad.

A laugh. Dry and crisp.

"Take a swing, boy, it might make you feel better."

Snake wrenched his arm from my hands, stalking forward. "You son of a bitch."

I lurched into his path, throwing my back against his chest. I wasn't going to let him hit his dad because I knew it wouldn't make him feel better, even if it felt good at the moment. Even if that was all he could think about right now.

I also wasn't going to let him get caught brawling in a public parking lot. There were some curious onlookers gathered around a window of the diner.

Snake's hands grabbed my biceps, like he was going to pick me up and forcibly move me out from in front of him, but I planted my feet.

And then I narrowed my gaze at his dad. At this perfectly ordinary looking man. "Go fuck yourself," I spat.

His eyes widened infinitesimally, like he was definitely not expecting that kind of vehemence from someone like me. Then his brow furrowed and he shoved his hands in the pockets of his jacket, turning to walk towards his truck. "Have fun at the funeral."

His wife looked once more at Snake with her red-rimmed eyes and then scurried along in his wake.

I could feel Snake's labored breathing on the back of my neck; feel the shaking of his hands where he still held me.

"Take me home," I said.

Snake had cut the engine and we sat in silence in the parking lot of our apartment complex.

His eyes were wet and his chest heaved, much as it had the whole drive.

Once again I was at a loss for words.

His hands were white-knuckled on the steering wheel.

After a couple more minutes of just breathing, he finally let go, hands falling to rest limp on the tops of his thighs.

"Sheenah, I never would have..." his words trailed off into the heavy silence of the car.

I nodded, but I wasn't ready to absolve him. Not yet.

"I think I need some space," I finally said, fingers picking at the fabric of my dress.

He scrubbed his palms over his face. "What are you talking about?"

"I just need some space." I pulled on the door handle, the metal creaking absurdly loud after so much silence. "I'm not some abused puppy you have to go around rescuing."

I left the rest of that sentiment hanging in the air between us. I didn't need him trying to rescue me because he couldn't rescue her.

"Sheenah..." His voice was a pained groan, eyes wild and still not focusing completely on my face.

I grabbed my bag and slid from the car, not looking back as I headed towards our apartment building.

CHAPTER NINETEEN

HURTS REALLY BAD

Three days without Snake and I was regretting my decision to ask for space. I ached for him in a way I had never felt before. My body missed the warmth of his pressed against me; my fingertips tingled with missing him.

The holidays were always hard on me, but this year just hit differently because I had someone and I pushed him away.

I didn't have to be alone on Christmas Eve again, but I had made that decision.

Vivien had invited me over to her mom's house like she usually did, but I didn't think I could stand watching her and Tobias revel in their happiness. I knew they weren't being happy and mushy *at* me, but I knew it would hurt all the same.

So, I worked and sewed and ignored calls from Grammy and drank too much sweet red wine.

Every time my phone pinged with a new message my heart stopped, hoping it was him.

Usually, it was just Vivi.

No fancy internship
for me booooo

> Aw, I'm sorry, friend.
> They don't know what
> they are missing!

I know, right?
Now I have to
succeed out of spite.

> Yeah! You don't
> need them.
> What's next after
> graduation now?

Her response did not come immediately. I knew how stressful it was to be asked about your after-graduation plans, especially now that the fall semester was over. There was only one more semester separating us from entering the post-college adult world. I knew Vivien didn't have a backup plan.

A reply finally came.

I...think I may be going with Tobias. He
got into a couple of grad programs out
of state. But nothing is really set in

stone yet. A bigger city could mean more opportunities for me.

I sent her some heart eyes.

> *I'm happy for you!*
> *You don't have to*
> *justify your*
> *decisions to me.*

It's not like I wasn't also planning on leaving the state, so I definitely couldn't begrudge Vivien the opportunity to do the same.

Love you, bestie!

> *Love you, too!*

More days and more pings and none of them Snake. He was frustratingly good at respecting boundaries.

I was so deep in my feelings that I said yes to Rayme's message about going out (*bitch, we're going to get drunk*).

I was tired of listening to his footsteps upstairs, tired of trying to catch a glimpse of him in the lobby or the parking lot. Another thing Snake was good at: apparently disappearing from shared common areas when you ask him for space.

I had never actually gone out for Christmas Eve and didn't really want to go to a bar, but I was tired of being alone with my own thoughts.

And Rayme sweetened the deal by picking a place within walking distance of my apartment.

I wore stockings, a snug, ribbed sweater dress, and a pair of heeled booties that I didn't wear much because they hurt my ankles.

I started walking at ten and made it to the bar by ten-ten.

The crowd at the door almost made me turn right around and leave. Who knew Christmas Eve was such a popular night to go drinking? In fact, my body was facing that direction, back towards the safety of home, when Rayme spotted me. They were with a whole gaggle of people I had never met before.

Rayme threw their arm around my waist and then did a rapid-fire introduction of everyone's name—which I could barely hear over the crowd and the music coming from the bar. So, I just did my best to smile and wave like I was here to have a good time.

Rayme hugged me tighter and grabbed my face to bring me down to their level. "Try not to be a stranger, okay? I'm really terrible at maintaining friendships. Out of sight, out of mind, ya know?"

My heart pounded, but I squeezed Rayme. That sounded very much like a goodbye. "I'll try."

And then I lost Rayme and almost everyone else as soon as the bouncer stamped our hands and let us into the building. I made a beeline straight for the bar, squeezing my taller frame between all the crushed bodies that were there first.

I ordered a hard cider and then bumped into one of Rayme's friends when I turned back around.

"Oof, sorry," I mumbled, cradling my bottle so it didn't spill as I crashed into his chest.

His hands came up and cupped my elbows. "My fault. Sheenah, right?"

I looked up; he was a couple inches taller than me. I recognized him from our very brief introduction but couldn't remember his name. I didn't like his closeness or the over familiarity of his hands on my arms.

I pulled back. "Sorry, I don't remember your name."

I had escaped his grasp, but he followed me back into the crowd anyway, hovering.

"It's Tyler."

"What?"

"TYLER," he hollered, causing several heads to turn in our direction curiously.

I had never been to this bar, so I wasn't familiar with its interior layout; I couldn't find a safe place to stand that wasn't in the middle of a bunch of people.

Tyler was still hovering, pushing his curly hair out of his eyes every once in a while.

"Do you want to dance?"

The answer to that was no but I couldn't really think of a good excuse not to. I had come to a bar, after all. I glanced around the bar for Rayme but couldn't see them, so I shrugged and took a deep swallow from my cider.

Tyler immediately had his hands on my waist, steering me a little deeper into the gyrating crowd of people. The music was nothing but a deep, vague roar in my ears.

Dancing with Tyler was about as titillating as tweezing my eyebrows. He didn't seem to know what to do with his hands, except keep them glued to my waist, and he didn't seem to know what to do with his hips except sway them slowly back and forth no matter the beat of the music.

His breath on the back of my neck, while unavoidable given our current position, was making my skin crawl. And not in a good way.

When his hand splayed across my stomach, I knew I'd finally had enough of pretending this was where I wanted to be or what I wanted to be doing.

I lurched out of his grasp and stumbled on my heels.

Tyler reached for me again. "Are you okay?"

"Yep, just...gotta pee!" I gave him a cheery wave on my way to what I hoped were the front doors.

Once out in the chill air, I felt like I could finally breathe again. I inhaled the crisp air while depositing my still half-full bottle into the nearest garbage can.

My walk home was quick and uneventful. I could just imagine the cozy pair of old sweats and popcorn that awaited me when I made it back to my apartment. I could just snuggle up and watch videos on my phone. Or I could just go to bed, which sounded like the much better option.

I pulled my phone out of my tiny clutch to check the time: 11:30. If I hurried, I could be in bed by midnight, which was my preferred bedtime.

I was attempting to shove my phone back in the tiny purse, so I wasn't paying much attention to the steps on the walkway that led up to the lobby. My ankle turned, impractical boot heel caught on the concrete, and down I went with a curse.

I landed on one knee, my palm, and my phone.

"Fuck."

My stockings were torn, the jagged edges of my knee peeking through. I gingerly touched the skin around the scrape only to wince because it *hurt*. My palm was scraped and bleeding too.

I grabbed my phone, slowly inspecting it for any damage. I could *not* afford to replace a phone right now. The screen protector was cracked, but that was an easier fix than the actual screen.

I sat forlornly on the steps, hand and knee aching, attempting to keep the tears at bay by squeezing my eyes shut. Maybe I should just cry. It'd been a few weeks since I'd had a good, cathartic sob. I didn't really relish the idea of having a mental breakdown on the steps of my apartment complex, but, hey, the year was almost over.

I took a deep breath and attempted to right myself, but both my ankle and my knee screamed out in violent protest and I plopped back down on my ass.

"Fuck," I said again, to the empty air.

With a sigh, I opened my text messages.

I cursed again when five minutes went by and Snake hadn't come to my rescue or replied to my text. I rubbed my cold nose. I probably deserved to be abandoned on the steps of our apartment building.

I took a picture of my damaged knee and sent it to him along with another plea for help.

Soon after, he swaggered out of the front doors in sweats, a hoodie, and fuzzy house slippers.

He towered over me, looking down at the mess that was me—bloody and smeared eyeliner and all—and cocked his head.

"I thought you didn't need to be rescued."

I sniffed, running a hand across my cold nose. "Yes, well. Shit happens."

He knelt down, his warm hands going to my knee and inspecting the damage. "In my professional opinion, I think you'll live."

"I think I broke my ankle."

His eyebrows raised.

"I mean, it hurts really bad."

"Can you stand?"

"I tried that. It didn't go well."

He exhaled, breath clouding the air. His hands were still on my knee, warmth seeping into my damaged skin. And feeling like solace. He wasn't meeting my eyes.

"I never would have let you see that," he said, eyes anywhere but on my face. "If I had known they were going to show up. I wouldn't have let you see that."

I put my hand on the back of his neck. "Snake, I know."

He nodded, but there was still a tightness in the set of his shoulders, in his mouth.

"Is your dad..." I trailed off, because it didn't feel right to finish my question and ask him if his dad had died yet.

"I told Mom to text me when I could show up for the funeral." His arms settled around my body. "Hold on."

I wrapped both arms around his neck as he scooped me up bodily from the ground with barely a huff.

"It's good that you're talking to your mom, at least," I said, trying to fill the silence. And then I nodded like I had imparted something profound.

Snake just grunted and we continued on in silence until we reached the stairs.

"Do you think you can hop? I can't carry you up the stairs." His cheeks were red.

I could have been embarrassed but I was honestly just continuously impressed by his ability to carry me around.

"I can hop."

He sat me down on my good leg and kept his arm around my waist for support. With his help, I hobbled up the stairs.

We didn't discuss it, but we headed for his apartment.

CHAPTER TWENTY
NOTHING LIKE HIM

Snake helped me hobble to the end of the bed, where he deposited me ungracefully.

He helped me take off the offending bootie and my ruined stockings. I wanted the actions to be terribly unsexy, but everything about Snake was hot. The way he moved, his gentle fingers as he pulled the fabric from my legs. My knee and ankle throbbed in agony, but tingly butterflies started in my stomach.

I hugged myself as Snake went to the kitchen and started the sink. "I'm so embarrassed. I've never wiped out like that before."

He came back with a damp rag and a surprisingly large and well-equipped first aid kit. "It happens to the best of us."

He dabbed at the blood on my knee, wiping it away with gentle strokes of his world-famous gentle hands.

"I'm surprised you came down," I said.

"Why?" He gave the scrape one more pass and then got out a large Band-Aid and antibacterial cream from the kit.

"Because I basically told you to fuck off after a deeply personal, probably traumatic event."

I had enough time to reflect on everything that had happened that night, everything said and left unsaid. And I had decided I had been the asshole. Snake probably needed some support, maybe even needed to talk it out with someone he liked and trusted. And I ran.

I was afraid. Not afraid of Snake's dad...afraid of the way I felt, afraid of the ease with which I threw myself in front of Snake to shield him from that man. I was a survivor, scrappy, my instincts were self-preservation. I had to put myself first because no one else in the whole world would do it. Then there was Snake. I was not afraid of him or his dad; I was afraid of myself, afraid of the burning emotion in my chest. Afraid that I would so easily sacrifice everything I was, everything I had, for him, again.

Snake dabbed the cream over the now-clean scrape and then pressed the bandage on, smoothing down the edges with his fingers.

His hands slid down my calf and he sighed. He picked up my foot and placed it on one of his thighs.

"I understand why you did. Can't say I blame you."

"Really? Because I barely understand why I did it."

He was massaging my sore ankle with his warm hands and it was absurdly hard to concentrate on the very serious conversation I was trying to have.

He pressed my toes back. "You think I think you're like my mom."

I gaped a little. "Oh."

"And you think I'm like my dad and that's terrifying."

"Snake, you're not—"

"I wanted to hit him, Sheenah. Probably would have, if you hadn't been there." His hands were still soft, but his words were rough with condemnation.

I couldn't take the head-ducking anymore. I reached down and grabbed his face, forcing him to meet my gaze.

His brown eyes were doe-wide, the soft shadows underneath more pronounced than usual. There was deep sadness there, and grief, years and years and years of it. His plump mouth was turned down at the ends, the expression creasing his cheeks, like he'd worn the same sadness for days.

I brushed my thumbs across the soft expanse under his eyes. "You are nothing like him." His hands stilled their rubbing. "You're the best man I know."

His eyes softened, shoulders visibly falling. "I doubt that." But the corner of his mouth quirked up.

I smiled. "Granted, my sample size is very small. The bar is basically on the floor at this point."

He surged upward until our lips met, the heat of his body seeping through mine like someone had dropped honey on my mouth.

Until his chest bumped my wounded knee and I winced.

He retreated with a small laugh. "You didn't even complain this much when I tattooed you."

I held my knee gingerly, giving it a betrayed glare. "It hurt less."

"How's the ankle?"

I gave it an experimental twirl and it twinged less. "Better."

"I'll get you some ice."

Snake went back to the kitchen and filled up two plastic baggies with ice cubes from the fridge. Then he helped me arrange myself out on his bed, my injured leg propped up with pillows while he carefully placed the ice baggies so they'd balance on my wounds.

He snuggled up next to me, one arm sliding beneath my neck so that I could nuzzle into the crook of his shoulder. We stayed locked like that for several long minutes, just quietly breathing.

"Oh!" He immediately dislodged me with his sudden movement. "I forgot. I have a present for you. Watch out." He maneuvered out from under me, grabbing my ice baggies and taking them back to the sink.

I felt my face go red. "Snake, you didn't have to. I...don't have anything for you."

He shrugged nonchalantly. "It's just something small." I heard him emptying the partially melted ice cubes into the sink. And then he grabbed a rectangular, festively wrapped present and brought it back to me on the bed along with a fresh baggie of ice.

Snake handed me the present and then pulled my ankle onto his lap. My fingers pulled at the neat edges of the wrapping paper, which was bright red and covered with snowmen.

"Go ahead. Open it." Snake's fingers massaged my ankle, while he gently laid the makeshift ice pack against it.

I ripped at the wrapping paper, suddenly feeling giddy. Aside from the odd gift from a friend every now and again, it had been a while since I'd received a Christmas gift on Christmas.

The snowmen gave way to reveal a yellow paperback: *The Collected Poems*, Sylvia Plath. My heart gave an uncomfortable lurch.

"The spine may be a bit cracked because I read some before wrapping," he said sheepishly to my foot. "She's good."

I thumbed through the creamy pages, the crispy, new-book smell sending a zip of serotonin right to my brain. "You really didn't have to."

He shrugged, the movement jostling my ankle that was still in his lap. "I almost didn't. After you abandoned me after the...display from my parents." His words were casual, tone admonishing nonetheless.

"I'm sorry," I said, pressing the book to my chest and deliberately pulling in a deep breath of air. "Thank you for giving it to me anyway."

He nodded. "For the record, I don't think you need to be saved." His eyes shifted down until he was staring at my knees. "I think you just need to be loved."

The tops of his cheeks had turned a ruddy shade of pink, a nascent smile taking shape on his mouth.

But my heart stopped, throat going dry from my quickened breath. One-handed, I reached down and grabbed the neckline of his hoodie, pulling his face towards mine.

I kissed Snake because I didn't know what I wanted to say. Kissed him like I was sorry. Kissed him like it was the first time and the last.

Chapter Twenty-One

SOMETHING EXTRAORDINARY

We continued on with our routine like the night with his parents and our subsequent break never happened.

There was a niggling suspicion at the back of my mind that maybe we should have spent more time talking about it and unpacking our feelings, but I pushed it aside in favor of just being with Snake. And enjoying our time together.

Time that felt like it was ticking down as if there was a stopwatch attached to it—a stopwatch only one of us could see.

We hung out in the shop, alternated sleeping over at each other's places; Snake helped me pack orders and clean out inventory, and gagged at the prices of my materials for the spring semester. Snake stopped by the coffee shop a few times on his way to work and my coworkers appropriately ribbed me for it while simultaneously *ooohing* over how hot he was.

We casually skipped Valentine's Day, mainly because Snake had to work late. He said it was an extremely popular date for walk-ins—couples looking to get matching tattoos and make questionable decisions with their names in romantic scripts. It was a big money day for the shop.

I didn't mind missing such a couple-centric holiday because then I could go on pretending in my fantasy world that we weren't a couple and that I wasn't lying to Snake by omission.

I quietly finished and submitted my application to GSAD at the beginning of March.

The insidious feeling that I was hiding something big and monumental from Snake grew and was a constant pressure in my chest, like a thorn in my shoe, or an itch I couldn't scratch, or a scab that I couldn't stop picking.

Guilt and shame spirals were so ingrained in my head—guilt over every impure action or sinful thought or short hem—that my guilt over Snake was almost a welcome addition. It was familiar. It was a feeling I knew how to handle.

I knew how to carry guilt—how to live with it.

Niyah, Austin, Snake, and I stood in the parking lot of Sabbath Ink, staring at one of the empty brick walls—empty save for the pieces of sketch paper Snake had taped in a neat little row.

It was a crisp early spring afternoon, chilly in the shade but warm under the sun. Our sketches fluttered in the slight breeze.

Austin wanted Snake to paint a mural on the side of the building that faced the road, to draw in and impress customers with the great talent of Sabbath Ink's artists.

I had a rare afternoon off so I was here for moral support and to offer my services—albeit extremely limited when it came to outdoor murals. I had never used the side of a building as a canvas before.

Snake crossed his arms, let out a little sigh, and eyed Austin, who was making a big show of minutely examining each of the proposed designs.

"Austin, dude, just pick one. We're never gonna get anywhere at this pace."

Austin rocked back on his heels, apparently racked with indecision. "I don't know, man."

I bristled. I had been up late with Snake the night before helping with the sketches, so I certainly felt a little miffed that he couldn't pick a design.

Judging by the crease that showed up between Snake's brows as he frowned, he was feeling the same way.

"Oh, for fuck's sake." Niyah swatted Austin on the arm and he let out an affronted gasp. She pointed. "The middle one. Horses, bourbon, goldenrod, perfect." Then she spun on her strappy wedges and headed back into the shop.

The middle one happened to be my favorite—a collage of ubiquitous Kentucky scenery and things in the shape of the state, with *My Old Kentucky Home* written in a curly script along the bottom. It was cute. Totally social media worthy. The influencers would be lining up for photo ops.

Austin swiped his hand across the scruffy stubble on his jaw. "Yeah, okay. Let's do it."

Snake clapped him on the shoulder. "Great. Give me your credit card."

"Excuse me?"

"I'm not buying all this shit. It's a business expense, dude."

With a grumble, Austin pulled out his wallet and handed over a shiny black card. "Keep it reasonable, okay?"

"You only want the best, right?" Snake snatched the card with a big grin, like a kid who had just been handed the keys to the candy store.

Snake and I had to stop at a couple different hardware stores to get all the supplies we would need for the mural—paint, brushes, rollers, tape, drop cloths, snacks, and of course a quick detour by the coffee shop for some pick-me-ups before we got started.

By the time we made it back to Sabbath Ink it was early afternoon and the sun had burned off some of the chill and morning dew from the air.

Snake immediately went to work prepping the area, opening paint cans and meticulously setting out his brushes.

I used one of the extra drop cloths to set up a makeshift tanning station on the warm asphalt. Not that I would tan at all, but the sun felt good on my skin. I kicked off my Crocs, pulled my bike shorts a bit higher, and sprawled out on the cloth with my iced coffee within grabbing distance.

It wasn't long before a shadow fell across my face. I squinted up to see Snake crouched above me. The sun was behind his head so I could only make out his wry grin.

"Comfortable?"

"Very."

"Can I get you anything? A little umbrella for your drink, maybe?"

I made a show of wriggling my shoulders on the drop cloth. "No, I'm good. Just let me know when you need help."

He snorted. "Don't overexert yourself."

"I won't!" I said cheerily, waving him off.

With a muttered grumble that made me smile, Snake went back to his work. I angled my body a bit more so that I could watch him.

He started by applying a generous layer of creamy white, I'm assuming so that the brighter colors would stand out against the brick once he got started on the main mural.

"You're doing a great job, babe!" I called out, giving him a thumbs-up from my prone position.

He shot me a dark look over his shoulder that made me giggle. I was lying in the sun, giggling and laughing like some infatuated teenager. Like someone who may have been more than infatuated. But that was a thought I didn't let take root in my chest, like some insidious vine. I couldn't let it bloom, let it grow, let it consume.

I still hadn't heard anything back from GSAD. Still hadn't told Snake about my application and my after-graduation plans. A part of me wanted to keep that information close to the chest because I was afraid of what would happen if I didn't get in. If they said no. I had been working towards this goal, this singular finish line for almost two years—ever since one of my studio professors gave me a GSAD brochure.

I had cut the pictures out—picaresque scenes of sprawling studio spaces; city squares with fountains; the snaking Savannah River; gaggles of laughing, smiling fashion students—and glued them to a vision board. Grad school was it for me, it was everything.

And I had done the one thing I'd swear I'd never do since Hunter.

I had fallen for a boy who turned my world on its axis.

I may have actually dozed off because the next thing I knew, Snake was flopping down beside me on the drop cloth.

"You are the worst personal assistant in the history of personal assistants," he said.

"I'm just here for moral support." I pushed my sunglasses up.

Snake had removed his shirt, so all his tattoos and smooth, taut, un-inked skin was on display, glistening with a light sheen of sweat. The afternoon had grown rather warm. As per usual, he had different colored paint splattered across his skin.

"Does being shirtless help you work?"

He grinned. "Distracted?"

I made a show of looking away. "Absolutely not."

He got to his feet and leaned over to grab my hand to help me up. "Come on. I need you to hold up my goldenrod references."

I Googled Kentucky goldenrod on my phone and held up the image results while he blocked out where the goldenrods would go on the mural. His brow was furrowed in concentration, a thin paintbrush with yellow bristles clutched between his teeth. He was too adorable. I couldn't resist.

My fingers grazed his exposed abdomen, the skin there impossibly soft yet the muscles underneath hard and rigid. They jumped at my touch, Snake's eyebrows drawing together even tighter, if that was possible.

"Now you're distracting me," he mumbled around the paintbrush.

I shrugged, but continued my lazy exploration, like I had never seen or touched him before.

Brushes clattered to the ground, and Snake's hot body crowded against mine until my back pressed up against the brick with a gasp. His arms bracketed my shoulders, nose immediately going to brush against the thready pulse in my throat.

It felt like he loomed over me, despite our height being the same. It was probably because the nearness of his body made my knees turn to quaking jelly and my insides to molten heat.

His bare chest brushed mine and my nipples hardened immediately, budding into rigid peaks, a tight, spiraling sensation that I could feel echoed in my core.

Time slowed to a crawl as we reveled in each other, breathing in one another like two people who couldn't get enough air. His plush mouth traced a blistering line up my throat and along my jaw.

"We're in public," I managed to gasp out, even as my fingers grasped at the waistband of his shorts.

His soft-as-silk gaze caressed down the lines of my body. "Not for long." Snake took my hand and his car keys from his pocket and led me around to the back of the building, where there was a steel rear door.

He grinned at me, eyes glinting, as he unlocked it and led me inside.

I had never been in this part of the shop; it must have been what was lurking behind the door marked "Employees Only" that you could see from the main shop. The space was small and included a private bathroom, washer, dryer, an industrial sink, and what looked like a small office.

We snuck into the empty office, Snake locking the knob and then turning to face me.

I was on my knees, tugging at his shorts.

"Sheenah, you don't—" His voice was a hoarse rasp.

"Shut up." I pushed a hand against his stomach as his hard cock bobbed free. Snake sagged against the door, all protests forgotten as I circled him with my free hand.

I massaged the hot, smooth flesh with my fingers, sliding my thumb across the already-leaking slit. Snake's heavy breathing labored above me, his body shaking.

He stopped me with a hand in my ponytail, tugging my head back. The eyes that met mine were dark with pleasure, glittering with it.

I wobbled to my feet, following the unspoken instructions in his gaze. His hot mouth and hands were on me, hands squeezing my ass and delving between my legs. He backed me up until my thighs hit the desk, freeing one leg from my shorts and underwear. His fingers found my clit, already slippery and swollen with desire.

I made a noise, but he caught it with his mouth. "You have to be quiet."

I bit at his lip.

Snake's free hand rummaged over the desk, knocking messy piles of paper to the ground.

"Someone will notice," I whispered in his ear, breath ragged.

He held up his hand, condom caught between his fingers. "Austin comes through sometimes."

I let out a peal of laughter and Snake shushed me, but he was laughing too, muffling the sound in my neck but I could feel his chest move with it.

Snake ripped the condom wrapper open with his teeth and managed to slip it on one-handed, since his other hand was still occupied.

I looped my arms around his neck, fingers tangling together behind his head as he gripped my hips; he nudged his stiff cock into the slick, wet heat of my body. The thrust was a measured, slow, agonizing, irrevocable slide of flesh on flesh that had us both keening.

One of his powerful hands gripped my thigh, while the other tugged gently on my ponytail. I nipped at his mouth, jaw, throat and locked my ankles, heels digging into the small of his back.

We were as close as two people could possibly be, and it didn't feel close enough. We were frantic, hips bucking, trying to immolate the other.

Snake gasped into my ear. "Fuck. Sheenah." He gasped my name like a devotional, like a prayer. "I never want to finish." He chuckled, the sound frayed and choked.

I dug my fingernails into his hot skin, lashes fluttering with each greedy thrust.

What if this is enough?

I let the thought simmer, even as I felt the coiling of an orgasm in my center.

What if being with Snake was enough? What if I didn't get into GSAD and that was okay because I had him and he had me—all of me. What if I let him?

Snake moved a hand between our bodies, thumb finding my clit again and I lost the thread of my rebellious thoughts under the wave of my orgasm. His body shuddered. We came together, gazes locked, sweaty forehead pressed to sweaty forehead.

His eyes were huge and luminous. Emotion flared there—something I couldn't, or wouldn't name. I closed my own eyes, letting the air out of my tight chest, even as my pussy still fluttered and clenched around him.

Snake brushed hair off my forehead, his touch gentle and soothing. "You're really something extraordinary," he said, voice almost wondrous, like he was discovering something new.

My tongue was heavy and sticky in my mouth. I just squeezed him with all the strength left in my quivering arms and legs. "We should get back before someone notices." My voice came out a quiet rasp.

He kissed my nose, soft length sliding from my body as he pulled away. The emptiness felt vast, like a yawning chasm between us, bigger, more profound than just cleaning up and righting our clothes after sex.

Snake straightened his shorts, running a preoccupied palm down his abdomen. He peeked out the door. "Okay, the coast is clear." He beamed a cheeky smile at me over his shoulder and then slipped out.

I leaned on the edge of the desk and took a minute to uncoil the knots tangled in my belly by taking deep breaths through my nose. Once I felt like I had my body and my emotions under control—my hands were no longer shaking—I followed Snake's path out of the office.

Turned out the coast was no longer clear.

Niyah was standing at the "Employees Only" entrance with her arms crossed loosely over her chest.

I froze, tugging on the hem of my shorts, which probably did nothing to make me look less conspicuous.

"Oh, hey," I chirped in a guilty falsetto, splotchy heat running down my neck.

She grinned at me, teeth sparkling white against her neon blue lipstick. "You have green paint in your hair."

I sheepishly grabbed the end of my ponytail. "Uh, thanks."

"Mm-hmm." She heaved the sigh of someone who definitely didn't get paid enough to deal with this, the sound following me as I fled out the rear door.

We finished the mural at about noon on the third day.

Austin was ecstatic. "I knew you wouldn't let me down, man."

Snake rolled his eyes. "Have I ever?"

But Austin missed that part because he already had his phone out and was muttering to himself about how the influencer girlies were going to love it.

He motioned for Snake to move in front of the mural. "Let's try it out."

"You're coming too," Snake said, grabbing my hand and tugging me towards the mural despite my protests.

But Austin was nodding his head. "Yes, good. Now pose." He huffed out a breath. "Okay, now pose like you like each other. What's wrong with y'all."

Snake was laughing, which made me grin, despite myself. I sidled a little closer to him and tangled our fingers together while Austin snapped pictures and directed like he was Annie Leibovitz.

"Perfect! That's the one!" he finally declared.

Snake's hand was warm and familiar in mine, a beatific grin breaking across his face. I knew Austin would post the pictures on Sabbath Ink's social media, so I would eventually get to see what he had captured.

I was almost afraid to look.

Austin put Snake back to work—he had a full afternoon of client appointments—so I returned to our apartment building alone.

I didn't know what prompted me to head for the mailboxes in the lobby.

Maybe because I hadn't checked the mail in over a week. Maybe because I was coming home alone for the first time in a long time. Maybe because I had been living a fairy tale for the last three days and it was time for a dose of reality.

The envelope was huge and white, folded around my other mail, the GSAD logo in the top left corner.

I had to sit down, the mail slumped loosely in my hands.

They wouldn't have sent me a rejection letter in such a big package.

So, I knew what it was.

Time for the fairy tale to end.

CHAPTER TWENTY-TWO

NEVER NEEDED YOU

Rose Hip Market Place was another fancy hipster joint that looked like it stepped right off a Pinterest board.

The outside of the building looked like an industrial warehouse, two sides of the building made of garage doors but with panes of glass so you could see the very chic brown, beige, and gold interior.

"Where do you find these places?" I asked.

"I Google 'cool date ideas,'" Snake said with a grin.

"Are you serious?"

"No, I asked Austin. Which is basically the same. He said the triceratops girl liked it."

"Triceratops girl?"

"Yeah, I forgot her name and they've already broken up. But she apparently said ten out of ten for this place. Verbatim."

We entered the candle shop and I was immediately assaulted by familiar low-fi coffee shop music and various candle-themed decor.

There were long wicks hanging from the ceiling over the quiet sitting area.

Instead of taking a seat to wait, Snake led us to the long bar where there were already a couple sets of different people. Maybe on their own weekend dates. We chose an empty section a couple seats down from the nearest person.

Snake tilted his body towards mine, our knees brushing under the bar, which gave us a semblance of privacy.

A middle-aged white woman with dark hair approached us immediately with a well-stocked charcuterie board and a carafe of water.

She set it down with a large smile. "Enjoy! I'll be right with you."

"Ooh, charcuterie!" I immediately helped myself to some salami and fancy cheese I couldn't identify.

Snake did the same. "Ten out of ten?"

"For the snacks only, definitely."

The white lady reappeared with a clap of her hands that startled us both.

"When you're ready, you can go pick out your containers and scents, and then we'll work on getting you ready to pour!"

She was gone again in a swish of hair and a clack of heels as she went to tend to the other patrons.

Snake shrugged but was barely concealing a grin. "Ready?"

I grabbed a handful of almonds to take with me. "Ready!"

The container and scent section was a whole wall of natural wood shelves. The containers varied from different glass shapes, to small metal tins, to fancy ceramic pots.

I picked up a white ceramic pot and rolled it between my hands. "Is there a price difference?"

"Don't worry about it." Snake picked up a circular shaped glass jar with an engraved leaf pattern. "Get what you want."

"Mm-hmm."

I grabbed a container that was identical to Snake's. He laughed. "Don't get too extravagant now."

We moved on to the scent section which was divided up into single-note fragrances and fancy pre-blended combinations like pumpkin pie. The fragrances had those little slips of paper testers like the fragrance aisle at a beauty store.

I looked at all the options, squeezing my jar. "I'm over-whelmed."

Snake had already picked a couple testers, holding them up to his nose like he'd done this before. "Just don't mix any weird ones and you should be fine."

"I think I'm going safe." I grabbed a sample for just plain berg-amot; the scent wafting up was a little fruity and a little spicy. I flipped over the card. "Oh, there are notes! Bergamot soothes the nerves and reduces tension. Lightens a heavy heart. Sold."

Snake chuckled, holding his own sample of lemon peel. "Why is your heart heavy?"

I froze, the bergamot sample up to my nose. Of course, he would catch on to that, wouldn't he? I couldn't sneak anything past this man, even when I did it subconsciously. I wasn't thinking about my little secret at the moment, but now it was the only thing racing through my mind.

It had been a week since I'd received my acceptance letter and welcome packet from GSAD. I had hidden the large envelope under my mattress, half convinced that if I just didn't look at it, it would disappear.

Maybe I'd get hit by a bus and then I wouldn't have to tell Snake at all. That option had some promise.

I shrugged, fluttering the bergamot sample. "You know, graduation is coming up and all." I winced internally. I wanted to steer the conversation away from after-graduation plans, not towards them.

His hand brushed the skin exposed by my backless jumper as he steered us back towards the candle bar. "Excited about that?"

I pretended to be very interested in my candle jar to avoid looking at him in the face. "It is what it is."

Now was the perfect opening to tell him about GSAD, if I was going to do it.

I was saved by our candle-making guide who had come back with a boxful of soy wax and a double boiler.

"Are you ready to melt?" she asked merrily.

I nodded vigorously. Anything to take the attention away from my guilty conscience.

We melted the wax, added our fragrances, placed our wicks—which took me four tries to get straight while Snake laughed and waited, having perfectly placed his wick on the first go.

It took at least an hour for our finished candles to harden, so we walked down the street arm in arm and had dinner at a local Vietnamese restaurant.

Snake was humming something under his breath by the time we made it back to his apartment. He set our candles down on the counter and thumbed open his phone.

I tilted my head quizzically, but then I heard the unmistakable beginning melody of Whitney's "I Wanna Dance with Somebody" coming out from the tiny speaker of his phone.

I froze in my tracks. "What are you doing?"

Snake grinned at me over his shoulder as the song continued, his shoulders shimmying with the beat. And then he started belting out the opening lyrics in a high-pitched soprano, his body in full girl-drunk-at-a-bar-on-karaoke-night mode, arms and hips swinging wildly.

I lost it, bending over in a full-on, side-aching laugh. His smile was radiant in the moody lighting of his apartment.

He grabbed my hands. "Dance with me."

I shook my head vehemently, but the lyrics were already coming out of my mouth. When Whitney started playing, you stopped what you were doing and danced. It was basically law.

Snake swung me around in a wild circle, both of us singing loudly and enthusiastically off-key. It was a good thing the downstairs apartment was mine and currently empty or I'm sure management would be hearing about our shenanigans.

Our bodies crashed together, Snake's strong arms bracketing my shoulders and lifting me off my feet to swing me around while I cackled.

He plopped me down in front of him, breathless.

"Come with me."

My head was still spinning. "Come with you where?"

His face was lit with enthusiasm. "This summer. There's this big tattoo convention in California." He shrugged. "I know it's kind of far away, but I want you to come with me. You'll be finished with school by then, right? It'll be like a vacation or something."

He was practically vibrating with excitement, while all I felt was an odd sense of numbness stealing over my whole body. This is what I had been waiting for. The other shoe to drop.

This man wanted to take me on vacation and, meanwhile, I was hiding my invitation to leave the state.

Something must have changed in my face, because his excited energy fizzled out and he rubbed his palms down my back. "Too soon? Is it too soon to ask you to take a trip with me?"

Yes, I wanted to say. It would have been the easy way out; a believable, ready-made excuse for why I couldn't go with him. I could maybe buy myself a few more weeks of ignorant bliss.

"Snake, I—"

Another song started auto playing on his phone, and Snake scrambled to grab his phone off the counter and turn it off. The motion put some distance between our bodies, which allowed me to take a gulp of air.

He slid his phone into the back pocket of his jeans. "Sorry. What were you going to say?"

We were still connected by our intertwined fingers and I glanced at our hands to avoid looking at his face. His palm was so warm.

"I applied to grad school. In Georgia."

"Okay? You applied so...?"

I dragged a breath in, throat tight. "I got in. I start in the summer. June."

The lines of his throat and jaw tightened as if he was working up what to say. Discarding his first reactions. "You got in."

"Yes. I'm going to move. To Georgia."

"You got in," he repeated, voice laced with confusion.

I shook our hands apart. He didn't understand, that was clear. I took a step back, finally looking up.

The boyish excitement and energy that had suffused his body only minutes ago had been replaced with confusion, hurt. His hand was still outstretched in the space where we used to be connected.

"I'm leaving," I said. My words came out firm even though I could feel a tremor in my hands.

He frowned, dropping his hand. "Were you ever going to tell me?"

"I'm telling you now."

"Only because I pushed the issue."

My heart did a little stutter as my brain worked to catch up. Was he trying to manipulate me? Was the invitation to the tattoo convention a ploy to get me to admit something he suspected? I had sworn I was done letting men have power over me.

I took another step back, closer to the door. "How dare you."

The condemnation left my mouth before I had even finished processing my muddled thoughts. Snake was not the one who had been keeping a secret.

Anger flashed briefly in his eyes. "How dare I what? Try to get you to be honest with me? I've had to fight for this every step of the way."

"I never asked you to do that!" My hand was on the door handle now. "I told you I didn't need rescuing."

"Could've fooled me." He crossed his arms over his chest.

My heart locked in my chest, lungs emptying out. "I never needed you, Isaac O'Connell."

At the mention of his real name—which I had only ever used during our most intimate moments—the color drained from his face, shoulders and chest deflating, stony look falling off his face.

"Sheenah, wait."

But I already had the door open. His hand landed on the frame, stopping me from shutting the door. The tendons in his forearm stood out, stark and angry. There was a controlled tightness in his body, in the shape of his lips.

He was pissed. And devastated. The two emotions oscillated across his face, in his eyes, in the hard set of his jaw.

I was just numb.

His dark gaze was gutted, spearing straight through me, a lance to my heart. "Sheenah. Fight with me. Fight for me. For us."

"This wasn't supposed to mean anything." The words were said quietly, almost a thought that was supposed to be kept to myself but slipped out anyway. Snake wanted me to be honest? Well, that was the truth.

His whole body stilled, mouth compressing into a bloodless white line. "And that's how you feel?"

No, it wasn't. But that was how I was supposed to feel so I could keep moving forward with my life. He had carved himself a place in my messy heart and I had to rip him out.

"Yes," I said, a burn flaring in my throat.

My stomach was a ruin of emotions, body shaking, but I stepped out the door and pulled it shut in my wake, swinging freely from Snake's slack fingers.

CHAPTER TWENTY-THREE
CAKE IS DELICIOUS

My new apartment was another studio in another collection of studios that was only a five-minute walk from the main design studio classrooms.

The apartments were tightly controlled by exiting and entering GSAD fashion students and it was only by sheer luck I had seen the post about a vacancy in the Facebook group—affectionately named the Fashion SADs.

It was the middle of June and I started grad school in three days.

I should be ecstatic, excited, overflowing with happiness and a sense of success and accomplishment.

I had escaped the small town I grew up in, the small town that had almost destroyed me. I had finally achieved what I had been working towards for the last couple of years.

And I was *happy*, I guess, but there was something else there. My excitement was tempered by longing, by regret, by all the feelings I had sworn I wasn't going to feel.

I had left Snake behind, but he still haunted me like a bruise that wouldn't heal.

"I must say, I am impressed by the closet space," Vivien said.

I had put Vivien in charge of closet and clothes organization, which was one of her strong suits. She was wearing an airy sundress, green hair pulled up into a dramatic ponytail as she surveyed her handiwork.

The closet space was huge. It was almost the size of three regular closets and had the added bonus of those built-in cubbies. One side was taken up by my regular clothes, organized by season and function, while the other side held my sample designs and supplies.

The Medusa was in a place of honor, fluffed up on my dress form in the corner.

Vivien propped her hands on her hips. "I think I'm done. Do you have any more boxes?"

I was sitting cross-legged on the floor, having just made my bed, which was also on the floor since I left my bed frame behind. I had left my couch and table and chairs behind too and had only taken what I could fit in Vivien's and my cars.

"That's the last of it." My heart thudded painfully as I pulled on the frayed edge of my jean shorts.

She must have heard something in my voice because she gave me a pointed look with her sharp-lined eyes. She stared at me for several heartbeats and I felt like she was looking right into my soul and trying to parse out the pieces. I became very invested in a spot on the popcorn ceiling.

"Let's go eat. I'm famished," she said finally, swinging a tiny purse over her shoulder and walking towards the door.

I scrambled to follow, grabbing my own bag and a pair of sandals.

The air outside was hot and humid and heavy; it stuck to your skin. I didn't mind the heat. Something about it burning my skin felt good.

Vivien waved a hand dramatically in front of her face and scowled. "It's fucking hot. I hate it."

I laughed and it was probably the first genuine laugh in weeks. I felt free; this felt right.

I tried to loop my arm through hers, but Vivien pushed me away. "Girl, you know I can't do skin on skin contact right now."

"You're real dramatic," I said, but I smiled as we wandered through the cobblestoned streets.

"I'm melting," she lamented. "I'm so glad we're moving north." She had on a pair of outrageously huge sunglasses, but I still knew she was observing the historic buildings and Spanish moss with disdain.

"So, it's settled, then? Where you and Tobias are going?"

"Pretty much. He accepted his invite to Chicago. He's going to be a TA. And insufferable now." A small, fond smile curved her hot pink lips.

It made my heart lurch uncomfortably.

"I can't wait to be cold," she continued gleefully.

I grabbed her hand despite her protests about the heat. "I'm gonna miss you."

She scoffed, but squeezed my fingers. "This isn't goodbye. Don't act like it's goodbye. We're just a few more hours apart, that's all."

We held hands, swinging arms obnoxiously, as we walked along the block, looking for something to eat.

We finally found a cute little shop that sold iced coffee and fancy sandwiches. Vivien waved my wallet away as she checked out.

"My treat. To celebrate!"

We took our way-to-expensive sandwiches and coffees to a shady concrete bench outside to people-watch.

I took a sip of my iced coffee. "Oh, that's good." My next gulp was larger and I had to resist the urge to chug it like it was water. "I'm definitely adding this place to my list."

Vivien nodded as she sipped her own coffee, eyes closed in bliss. "Are you going to miss your coffee discount?"

"Discount yes, customer service no. I think Alanna almost cried when I told her I was leaving. She offered to call the store manager down here and get me a job."

Vivien raised her eyebrows. "You said no?"

"I might still change my mind. But I'd like to see if I can find something closer to school or to fashion, at least. I'm so tired of the hustle, you know?"

She tipped her cup towards me. "Preach."

"Oh, and I get to take out student loans and they're giving me refund money."

"You know you have to pay that back, right? It's not free money."

"Yeah, well, not if the government collapses."

Her face crinkled with amusement. "One can only hope." She took a bite of her sandwich and I sipped happily on my coffee. "You sound like you have everything figured out."

There was definitely an undercurrent of *something* lacing her seemingly innocuous observation. It didn't take a rocket scientist to connect it to the look she gave me before we left the apartment.

"I do," I said, with more confidence than I felt.

I *should* have felt confident. I had a place to live, I had already met some of the people in my cohort, I had scoped out and made a list of cool places to eat and shop, I had a small buffer of savings and once my federal student aid was posted, I'd have a fat little refund check to help with materials and supplies and anything else I needed for school. I had some breathing room, *finally*, so why did it feel like I couldn't draw air without my chest hurting?

Vivien swirled her cup, ice clinking against the plastic, and pinned me with a look. "Okay, out with it. I've waited long enough. Entirely too long, for my liking."

"Out with what?" My shoulders drew down and I knew I was hunching in on myself. As if that could protect me from the truth.

"What happened with Snake?"

"Oh, that," I said in such a small, wavery voice.

"Yes, that. Don't think I don't know you, Sheenah Marie. You've been putting on a very good show, I'll give you that, but now I want you to tell me what happened."

I rubbed my cup between my hands, the cold making my palms red. "It didn't last. It wasn't supposed to last. I told you that before. I told you that I wasn't going to lose focus."

And I hadn't, not when it came down to making the final choice. I was where I wanted to be. Wasn't I?

I hadn't seen or heard from Snake since I told him to leave me alone for the second time. I had spotted the back of his head briefly in the parking lot a couple days before I moved out, but I had been too scared to call out. Afraid he wouldn't look back.

I didn't mention that I had absconded with one of Snake's Sabbath Ink shirts and wore it to bed until it no longer smelled like him.

Vivien made a quiet snorting noise. "You don't seem happy about it."

I let out a breath of air, my whole body physically deflating. I let my gaze wander off into the distance, into the throngs of people crowding the walkways and weaving their way through shops.

I had been so busy, so consumed, with the logistics of moving and finding a new apartment and finalizing my admission, that there hadn't been much room for anything else. I preferred it that way. I had done that on purpose. I didn't want to have the space to pause and rethink my decisions.

Because then the fear and the doubt crept in. The uncertainty. The worry that I had made the wrong choice.

"I am happy," I said. "This is everything I've always wanted. This is my dream." Even as I said the words, they rang hollow and false and I couldn't meet Vivien's gaze.

"Dreams can change."

I shook my head. "Not mine."

"You could have both, though. Long-distance relationships are still a thing, you know." She shook her cup again.

I just gaped like a fish. Was that an option? Would Snake have been down for a long-distance relationship?

"It's a nine-hour drive."

"Airplanes."

I crossed my arms and faced her, suddenly angry. "Why are you doing this? You, of all people, telling me I should have chosen a boy over my dream. Over my career? My future?"

She held up a palm in surrender, but there was still a sly smirk on her mouth. "I'm just saying you might not have had to choose. That's all."

"We're not all you, Vivien. Some of us can't have our cake and eat it too."

She shrugged, but I had a feeling I hadn't convinced her that I was okay, no matter how angry my words were or how much I glared at her.

"Cake is delicious," she said, brows raised as she sipped on the dregs of her iced coffee.

I turned away, anger fizzling out as quickly as it had ignited.

I didn't have time for regrets or second-guessing or missed connections. They were like a tidal wave; if I let them in, even only for a second, they would rise up and drown me.

CHAPTER TWENTY-FOUR

SEX AND ICE CREAM

Vivien hit the road about an hour later which left me to my own devices for the rest of the afternoon.

I switched out my sandals for a pair of sneakers and started my thrifting journey. I had already compiled a list of possible peddler's malls and antique stores and started from the farthest away from my new apartment and worked my way closer.

I was still empty-handed at my second store when I spotted them: a pair of sturdy French country chairs. They were solid and had wide seats. The fabric needed to be replaced but that was something I could do easily. Reupholstery was nothing, considering the excellent shape they were in.

I ran my hand along the back of one of them, testing the wiggle of the legs and trying not to look too interested because I noticed an older lady seemed to be watching me examine them.

I was about to walk away when she said, "Lovely, aren't they?"

I smiled at her. "They are."

She finished styling a bookcase and came over. She was wearing light wash jeans and a T-shirt that said Fee's French Finds across the chest. She must be Fee.

"Great shape too. You can't really find pairs like this that are in such good condition." As if to illustrate her point, she sat down in one, crossing her legs, strappy sandals dangling off pedicured toes.

I sat in the other, running my hands along the fabric on the arms. "How much?"

"Five hundred for the pair."

I didn't mean to, but a snort escaped me anyway. "Absolutely not." They were pretty, but not five hundred dollars' worth of pretty. "Two hundred."

The woman narrowed her eyes but there was no malice there. She was just sizing me up to see how hard I would haggle.

"Three hundred."

"Two hundred and fifty."

"Two seventy-five and I'll throw in a table." She gestured towards a small tiered white-washed end table.

"What's wrong with the table?"

She shrugged. "I haven't been able to sell it by itself. People seem to want two of them."

"It's a deal, then."

She grinned and we shook hands.

I wasn't sure how I was going to fit two chairs into my tiny car but Fee solved that problem too for thirty bucks and delivered the chairs to my apartment in the back of her truck.

Buying two chairs and an end table was probably not the most practical decision—seeing as my bed was still on the floor—but they made the room feel slightly homier.

I put both chairs by the large window, where I could perch and watch the sun go down on the street.

I had bought a new sketchbook to mark the occasion, to signal the fresh start. I propped it on my knees and drew the Savannah skyline at dusk.

It wasn't enough.

It wasn't enough to fill the empty ache in my chest.

It was hot in Georgia, hotter than I was used to, and the sounds at night were unfamiliar. I hadn't really been sleeping well and tonight was no different.

I woke up sometime in the middle of the night with the sheets tangled around my bare legs, ceiling fan whirring and doing its best.

The air was still heavy with heat and silence.

I grabbed my phone off the side table to check the time. It was after two a.m. Then I noticed the text messages.

I don't want to startle you or creep you out, but I need you to check your door.

I'll wait for as long as I can, but after…an hour…I'm going to assume you're just asleep and not ignoring me.

I was suddenly awake and alert, sleep just a distant memory.

The text had come in ten minutes ago.

I bolted from the bed and ran to the door without taking a breath.

I flung it open and Snake was there.

He braced both hands on the doorframe and leaned forward slightly, muscles in his arms bunching and coiling. His smell—God, his smell—sharp and crisp and familiar filled my nostrils. His liquid brown eyes took me in from head to beige underwear to bare toes. They darkened with desire as he swept down my exposed legs like he'd never seen me before. His tongue darted out to wet his lips while he held me trapped in his hot gaze.

Then he grinned. "That's my shirt."

I tugged on the hem of his shirt, which was barely covering my underwear, and tried not to rub my thighs together. "How did you know where to find me?"

He leaned further in the door and my body felt drawn to him like a magnet. It took everything I had not to just leap into his arms.

"Vivien messaged me and said you might have some doubts."

I frowned. "Vivien is a menace."

"Do you want me to go?"

I tried to do the math in my head but math was never my strong suit and I kept getting distracted by Snake's biceps. Vivien probably messaged him before she even left Savannah and Snake had dropped everything to jump in the car and drive down. Just like that.

"You came all this way. You might as well come in."

I stepped back and let him in my new apartment, our arms brushing, the brief contact breaking goose bumps out along my arms.

He surveyed the apartment with his hands on his hips like he was a mother dropping his kid off to college for the first time.

"Cozy." He looked pointedly at the bed on the floor. "Sparse, but cozy."

I scrubbed my palms over my face. His presence was making my whole chest ache. It was easy enough to convince myself that he didn't mean anything, that our time didn't mean anything to me, when we were almost six hundred miles apart, separated by my stubbornness and sheer force of will.

But now we weren't.

Now he was here and acting like nothing had happened. Like I hadn't unceremoniously dumped him and left without looking back.

"Hey…" He gently grabbed one of my wrists and pulled my hand away. "Don't do that."

Then I realized I was crying and my palms were wet.

"Sorry." I laughed. "I didn't mean to do that."

"You don't have to apologize."

He still held my wrist loosely between his fingers, his skin burning mine.

"I think I do."

I couldn't take it anymore.

I closed the space between us, wrapping my arms around his torso and crushing our bodies together. I kissed him, hard, his sweet mouth melding to mine like no time had passed at all.

His arms wrapped around me, one hand gripping the back of my neck and the other pressing into the small of my back. He broke the kiss, burying his nose in the soft spot between my throat and shoulder. He inhaled, like he was drowning, like I was air. And then he kissed that spot tenderly, sucking at my skin.

The sensation made me moan, head falling back and body rubbing against his. The hand at my back skimmed down until he was gripping a handful of my ass. His hard erection pressed into my stomach and I rubbed against him futilely, nipples aching. It wasn't enough. It wasn't ever going to be enough.

When I reached down and squeezed his cock, he groaned, his whole body shaking. "Fuck. Sheenah, we need to talk."

I squeezed harder until he hissed and his hips bucked. "I don't want to talk right now. Just take me to bed. Please."

A growl rumbled low in his throat but he hiked me up into his arms, hands under my ass while I held on to his neck.

He carried me to the bed, bearing me down with a knee between my legs, pressed against my aching core.

His hands slid up my T-shirt, warm palms covering my breasts while he went back to kissing my throat. He sucked and plucked my nipples and ground his knee against my pussy until I was keening with need, my head thrashing on the bed.

He took my earlobe between his teeth, breath warm on my neck. "So pretty. Tell me what you need." One of his hands slipped down to rub my clit from over my underwear. "Tell me what this pretty pussy needs."

The heat flooded my face, cheeks burning, but I was gasping, knees trying to close around his hand, but he kept me spread apart with his body.

"You. I need you."

His fingers rubbed the wet fabric. "Be more specific, sweetheart."

I opened my eyes to look at his face. His cheeks were flushed, eyes so dark they almost looked black in the dim lights from the street, his lips curved in a wicked grin.

His fingers teased me, the touches soft and not at all effective.

"I need you to fuck my pussy."

He hummed, that sound spearing something down deep inside me. And then he finally moved his hand inside my underwear, index finger sliding up my clit with sure strokes.

I moaned, the sound low and drawn out, pressing myself hard against his hand. He didn't make me wait. He rubbed my clit firmly while my hips bucked, the hot pressure of an orgasm building in my lower belly. Then he impaled me with two fingers, thumb on my clit with fast strokes, until I broke apart, pussy clenching over his fingers, coating them in my desire.

He buried his nose in my throat while I rode out the crashing orgasm on his hand, a sheen of sweat breaking out on my forehead.

My pussy hadn't even stopped fluttering before he yanked my underwear off, grabbed my hips and rolled me over.

He leaned over me and whispered, "Now, I'm going to fuck you."

He pulled my hips up, so that I was kneeling on the bed, weight braced on my forearms, the core of me exposed to the air. I shook with anticipation.

There was only a moment's pause while Snake discarded his own clothes and pulled on a condom, but then he was pressing the thick head of his cock against my soft entrance.

His hands rubbed gently up my flanks, but then he thrust inside me with one snap of his hips.

Snake's pace was a thundering pound that rattled my bones, turned my legs into jelly, and had me clenching desperately around him. He fisted his hand in my hair, causing me to arch my back with a cry so he could go deeper.

He wasn't holding anything back.

And I didn't want him to.

I wanted him to absolve me, forgive me, break me, fuck me normal. Anything that would make the fear and the uncertainty go away. Anything to make the hurt, that soul-deep ache, go away.

Another bone-deep orgasm ripped through me and I buried my face in my arms as Snake chased his own release inside me.

Snake was half naked in my kitchen rummaging through the cabinets.

"You don't have any food."

"I just moved here."

He gave a disappointed shake of his head and pulled his phone out of the pocket of his shorts.

I had wrapped myself up in my comforter but I sat up to look at him. "What are you doing?"

"Ordering food."

"It's almost four in the morning. There's nothing open."

He held up a finger, eyes not leaving the screen. "Ah, maybe not where we come from but we're in the big city now."

I know he probably didn't mean it, and it was just him making conversation, but the way he said "we're" made my stomach flutter.

I took a second to glance at my own phone and noticed I had a text message notification. It was from Vivien.

I hope by now Snake has made it to Georgia and you have thoroughly said hello. You can be mad at me for a little while for meddling. You know I'm not a meddler. But I consider it my duty as your best friend not to let you self-sabotage. You deserve the chance to be happy and Snake is too respectful to just go after you and make you see reason. So, I helped. Enjoy eating your cake. Wink wink.

She ended the text with a series of winking and kissy face emojis.

I couldn't help but smile. After our enthusiastic hello, I didn't know if I even had the energy left to be mad at her.

Snake plopped down beside me on the bed, propping his chin on my shoulder. "Who's made you smile?"

I put the phone back on the bedside table. "Just Vivien. She sent the longest text message in the world."

I felt him smile against my bare shoulder. "Don't be mad at her."

I let out a long-suffering sigh. "I'm not."

"Can we talk now?"

I shook my head, playing with a loose thread in the blanket. "Can we eat first?"

He conceded without a fight and while we waited for our food, I told him about my first classes and walked him through my sketchbook. I showed him my summer line for my shop, which was going to be a set of strappy sundresses with coordinating bangles and dramatic earrings.

He tilted his head thoughtfully. "I think you can make them longer."

I turned the sketches toward me. "The earrings?"

"Yeah. If you're gonna go big, go all the way."

I grabbed a stray pencil that I kept by the bed for emergencies. I added a few more beaded tiers to the earrings. On the average person, when worn, they'd lay almost to the top of a dress.

"Like this?"

"Indeed."

The bell rang and Snake went to answer it because I was still completely naked under the covers and he at least had shorts on.

Turns out the food Snake ordered was just dessert: warm chocolate chip cookies topped with fudge and ice cream.

We ate our ice cream in silence and watched as the first rays of dawn began creeping over the horizon.

I had a couple days of just hanging out before the term officially started, so I could spend the day sleeping in. Surely Snake had other things to do? Surely leaving wasn't just that easy.

I finished my dessert and set it aside on the floor. "Look, I appreciate you coming all the way down here, but—"

"No buts," he interrupted. "If you think I drove all this way just for sex and ice cream, you'd be wrong."

"Then why?"

"For you."

I shook my head even as butterflies started rioting in my stomach and my heart constricted in my chest.

Snake put his own dessert away and grabbed my hands, forcing me to look at him with fingers under my chin.

"I understand why you dumped me, *again*, I get it. I really do. I understand your reasons, but it's not good enough."

That caused me to frown and sputter, ready to fight him and say that of course it was good enough. They were my reasons. And how dare he tell me they weren't good enough.

I opened my mouth to tell him off, but he put a finger over my lips. "Nope. I'm not done yet." He gave me a little smile and squeezed my hands gently. "I left you alone because I thought you'd come to your senses. You're more stubborn than you look." His mouth twisted wryly. "I didn't want to disrespect your boundaries or chase you if you didn't want to be chased. Maybe that was my mistake."

"Snake—"

"No, I need you to listen. I'm fighting for us. I'm going to do whatever it takes, follow you wherever you need to go. You're my home, Sheenah." His face grew solemn, eyes bright and sincere. "Sheenah, I lo—"

I ripped my hand from his and slapped it over his mouth, slapped the words right out of his mouth.

His eyes went startled and then he frowned, thick brows creasing.

My heart was hammering against my ribs, so fast I felt almost like I had run a race. My breathing was shallow, chest heaving.

"Don't," I croaked. "Don't say it if you don't mean it. Snake, please, don't."

He gently pulled my hand away, light red marks blooming in the shape of my fingers on his cheek. "One: ouch. Two: I love you."

The air left my lungs in a furious whoosh, my shoulders sagged, the room tipped. Was I about to faint?

Snake must have had the same thought because he grabbed my shoulders, steadying me, and brought our gazes together again.

He was smiling and he kissed the tip of my nose. "I love you."

I tried to focus on his face again but it was all a blur of features, like a Picasso. "What about your job? What about your life? What about..."

I trailed off because I couldn't think of anything else, couldn't even string any more words together.

"I love you. And I've already quit."

And then the whole room went black as I passed out.

EPILOGUE

Snake's new shop was nestled in the heart of downtown historic Savannah, next to galleries and boutiques under multicolored awnings, with a scenic view of the river. The space was not as sprawling as Sabbath Ink, but it always seemed busy and full of out-of-towners getting commemorative tattoos.

Snake wasn't buddy-buddy with his new boss like he was with Austin—who apparently threw the biggest hissy fit ever when Snake quit—so I had to actually pay for my appointment this time. Snake still cut me a deal and didn't charge me quite his normal hourly rate.

Girlfriend perks, I guessed.

I was facedown on Snake's table, while his warm hands worked on the back of my thigh. He was finally finishing my tattoo.

"How come you can sit here and have me drive tiny needles into your skin without flinching but you had a panic attack when I told you I loved you?"

I smiled into my arm. "If I knew, I would tell you."

Snake had taken my whole "passing out during his declaration of love" episode with grace and good humor. I had only blacked out for like a second, but he'd still hovered over me like a mother hen, getting me ice and water.

And then...he just never left.

We had been living together for two weeks and it felt like the most natural thing in the world. I had never lived with someone before, so I didn't really know what to expect from the whole cohabitation situation. But Snake was courteous and didn't take up much space. He hadn't even made me sacrifice any space in the closet.

It was nice to have someone to share small moments with. To talk about my day and how my classes were going and my art. He helped me with design homework and we would paint together, which usually resulted in us both naked and sated. Snake was usually out working later than me, and I'd smile every time he came home and wrapped his body around mine in the dark.

Home.

It went from being my apartment to our home in a span of time that should have made me wary, maybe even concerned.

A little voice in my head liked to whisper that I didn't deserve to be this happy, that it was all going to come crashing down on my head when I least expected it.

I could live waiting for the other shoe to drop or I could live trusting my instincts for once. I knew my trauma was not all magically gone, because that's not how trauma worked, but I trusted Snake. I trusted we could battle our demons together.

And I trusted myself. And I *liked* myself. I liked the version of me that was happy with him.

"You're all done." I felt him wiping down my leg. "Do you want to see it?"

I shook my head. "If it's bad, it's too late now."

"It is not bad," he grumbled, clearly insulted.

He wrapped me up and helped me down off the table and gave me my bag while I adjusted my shorts. Then he walked me to the door with his warm hand on the small of my back.

I turned around to kiss him. "Are you working late tonight?"

"Not too late. About ten." He kissed me back, lips warm in the dry heat.

"I'm going to cook dinner."

His eyes widened in shock and then narrowed mischievously. "Should I pick up a backup on my way home?"

I swatted at him. "Don't you dare. You have to eat whatever it is and in whatever condition it's in."

He grabbed my hip, hand dangerously close to my ass for a public sidewalk. "I'll eat something."

"You have a filthy mouth." I flushed, heat traveling down my neck and across my chest. My heart hammered. I grabbed his chin, much like he had that night two weeks ago. "Hey, I love you."

He smiled, huge and goofy, his whole face lighting up like a kid on Christmas morning. Like a man who'd gotten everything he ever wanted.

I could feel my flush deepening as he just stared at me for several heartbeats before picking me up and spinning me around on the sidewalk.

"You didn't pass out that time."

I laughed, loud and carefree and unashamed, my arms tight around his neck. "No, I didn't." I kissed him again, our noses brushing. "I love you."

My chest was light, unburdened, and I felt like giggling, like screaming to the world, to every passerby on the sidewalk, that I loved this man.

I settled for a hand on the back of his neck, his body pressed to mine, warm under the Savannah summer sun.

Afterword

Thank you for reading *What Kind of Fool*!

Reviews are a great way to support authors, and I would appreciate you leaving one on a retails site or anywhere else on the internet. If you post about the book on social media, you can use the hashtags #wkof or #whatkindoffool so I can find, like, and share the post!

Be sure you're following me for updates about the next Penn Warren book, *Trouble With the Truth*.

xoxo,

jessica

About the Author

J.L. Minyard is the not-so-secret pen name of award-winning young adult author Jessica Minyard. Jessica is an author, poet, ISTJ, Sagittarius, and boy mom who lives and writes from the bluegrass.

For freebies, sneak peeks, and other updates, sign up for her newsletter: https://www.subscribepage.com/jessicaminyard

Follow her on social media:

facebook.com/jessicaminyardbooks

instagram.com/callmeshashka

tiktok.com/@jessicawritesromance

amazon.com/author/jlminyard

Minyard's Minions